A DATE WITH
THE ICE PRINCESS

BY
KATE HARDY

MILLS &
BOON

First published in Great Britain 2013
by Mills & Boon, an imprint of Harlequin (UK) Limited.
Harlequin (UK) Limited, Eton House,
18-24 Paradise Road, Richmond, Surrey TW9 1SR

© Pamela Brooks 2013

ISBN: 978 0 263 89903 0

Harlequin (UK) policy is to use papers that are natural, renewable and recyclable products and made from wood grown in sustainable forests. The logging and manufacturing process conform to the legal environmental regulations of the country of origin.

Printed and bound in Spain
by Blackprint CPI, Barcelona

Kate Hardy lives in Norwich, in the east of England, with her husband, two young children, one bouncy spaniel, and too many books to count! When she's not busy writing romance or researching local history she helps out at her children's schools. She also loves cooking—spot the recipes sneaked into her books! (They're also on her website, along with extracts and stories behind the books.) Writing for Mills & Boon® has been a dream come true for Kate—something she wanted to do ever since she was twelve. She's been writing Medical Romances™ for over ten years now. She says it's the best of both worlds, because she gets to learn lots of new things when she's researching the background to a book: add a touch of passion, drama and danger, a new gorgeous hero every time, and it's the perfect job!

**These books are also available in eBook format
from www.millsandboon.co.uk**

CHAPTER ONE

'ABIGAIL, AS YOU'VE only been with the team for a few weeks, I know it's a bit of an ask,' Max Fenton, the duty consultant, said, 'but Marina's put a lot into setting up the promise auction next weekend. So I was wondering if you might be able to donate something?'

Abigail knew that the quickest thing would be to ask her dad and his band to sign a photo and some CDs. Or offer tickets and a backstage pass to Brydon's next tour. Except she'd learned the hard way not to mention that her father was the rock guitarist and singer Keith Brydon, founder of the group that bore his surname. Or that her flat had been bought with the royalties from 'Cinnamon Baby', the song he'd written for her the day of her birth. It might be a quick win, but it'd make her life way too complicated.

She could simply say no, but that would be mean. The promise auction was raising funds to buy equipment that the department badly needed. And she did want to help.

'I, um…OK,' she said. 'What did you have in mind?'

'Max, are you pestering our poor new special reg?' Marina asked, coming to stand with them and sliding her arms round her husband's waist.

'On your behalf, yes.' He twisted around to kiss her.

The perfect couple, Abigail thought, clearly so much in love. And even though she knew she was better off on her own, she couldn't help feeling slightly wistful at the love in their expressions. What would it be like to be with someone who loved her that much?

Marina rolled her eyes. 'Ignore him, Abigail. You honestly don't have to do anything.'

Which left her on the outside, Abigail thought. Where she'd always been. Would it be so hard to be part of the team for once? 'No, I'd really like to help,' she said. 'What sort of thing do you suggest?'

'Really?' Marina looked faintly surprised, then delighted. 'Well, other people have offered things like dinner out, or cleaning for a day, or a basket of stuff.' She paused. 'Maybe you could offer some cinema tickets with popcorn and a drink thrown in, or something like that.'

'Or a date. That'd be a good one,' Max chipped in.

'Shut up, Max. You're not meant to be pressuring her. A date's not a good idea. You know what—' Marina stopped abruptly and put a hand to her mouth, looking horrified.

Abigail could guess why. And what Marina had been going to say. 'It's OK. I know people call me the ice princess,' she said dryly. 'It was the same at my last hospital.'

'People don't mean to be unkind.' Marina looked awkward. 'It's just that…well, you keep yourself to yourself. It's quite hard to get to know you.'

'Yes.' There wasn't much else Abigail could say. It was true. She did keep herself to herself. For a very good reason. Once people worked out who she was, they tried to get close to her so they could get to meet her father—not because they wanted to get to know her better. Been there, done that, worn the T-shirt to shreds. She blew out a breath. 'OK, then. I'll offer a date.'

'Please don't feel that we've pushed you into this,' Marina said. 'If you'd rather offer a basket of girly stuff or some cinema tickets, that'd be just as good.'

It was a let-out. But Abigail was convinced, whatever Marina said, that her colleagues would think even less of her if she took it. 'The date's fine,' she said.

Relief flooded Marina's expression. 'Thank you, Abigail. That's fabulous. I really appreciate it.'

And maybe, Abigail thought, this would be a new start for her. A way of making friends. Real friends for once. Something she'd always found so difficult in the past.

The alternative—that she'd just made a huge, huge mistake—was something she didn't want to think about.

Friday the following week was the night of the auction. The room was absolutely packed; all the emergency department staff who weren't on duty were there, along with people Abigail half recognised from other departments that she'd met briefly while discussing the handover of patients.

Max Fenton and Marco Ranieri, two of the department's consultants, had a double act going on as the auctioneers. And they hadn't spared themselves from the promise auction: they'd both put themselves up as household slaves for a day, and driven each other's price up accordingly.

Abigail bid successfully on a pair of tickets to a classical concert, and then it was her own promise up for auction.

A date.

Adrenalin prickled at the back of her neck. Why on earth hadn't she thought to ask someone to bid for her at the auction? She would've funded the cost herself, and it would've gotten her out of an awkward situation.

Still, she was the ice princess. Hardly anyone would be interested in a date with her, would they?

Except that Marco and Max seemed to be on a roll, really talking her up.

Abigail could barely breathe when the bidding reached three figures.

And then a male voice drawled, 'Five hundred pounds.'

Oh, for goodness' sake. That was a ridiculous sum. And the only reason she could think of that the man would pay that sort of money for a date with her was because he'd found out who she was.

Please, please, let her be wrong.

She held her breath, not quite daring to turn round and look at whoever was bidding. Not wanting to make eye contact.

Everyone else in the room seemed to be holding their breath, too.

And then Max said easily, 'Do we have an increase on five hundred pounds?'

Silence.

'OK, then, that's a wrap. Thank you. One date with Dr Abigail Smith, sold to Dr Lewis Gallagher.'

Lewis Gallagher?

Abigail's brain couldn't quite process it. Lewis Gallagher, special registrar in the emergency department, was the one man in the hospital who really didn't have to buy a date. Women queued up to date him because he was a challenge. Every single one of them seemed to believe that she'd be the one to make him review his 'three dates and you're out' policy. And, from what Abigail had heard, every single one of them failed.

Except her. Because when Lewis had asked her out last week, she'd said no.

And now he'd *bought* a date with her.

Oh, help. She needed some air. Time to think about how she was going to get out of this.

Except it was too late, because Lewis was standing beside her.

'Move to me, I think, Dr Smith,' he said softly, brandishing the certificate Marina had got her to sign for the auction—the promise of a date.

'Five hundred pounds is a lot of money. Thank you for supporting the auction.' She lifted her chin. 'You get a date, but don't expect me to end up in your bed.'

He laughed. 'What makes you think that's what I had in mind?'

His reputation. Colour rushed into her face. 'So why did you buy a date with me, Dr Gallagher?' *Because he knew who she was?*

He shrugged. 'Because you said no when I asked you.'

Ah. Because she'd challenged his ego. She relaxed. Just a little bit.

He held her gaze. 'And now you don't have an excuse to say no.'

'Maybe I just don't want to go out with a party boy.' She'd recognised his type the first time she'd met him. Handsome, wonderful social skills—and shallow as a puddle.

Not her type.

At all.

Lewis gave her the most charming, heart-melting smile she'd ever seen in her life. She'd just bet he practised it in front of a mirror.

'Maybe I'm not the party boy you think I am,' he said. 'Want to know where we're going?'

'I haven't decided yet,' she said. And she almost winced at how haughty and snooty she sounded. This was ridiculous. She didn't behave like a spoiled diva. That wasn't who she was. Abigail Smith was a quiet and hard-working doctor who just got on with whatever needed to be done.

Yet Lewis Gallagher made her feel like a brat, wanting to throw a tantrum and stamp her feet when she didn't get her own way. And she couldn't understand why on earth he was affecting her like this.

'Newsflash for you, princess. I bought a date with you. So you don't get to decide where we're going.'

Shut up, Abigail. Don't answer him. Don't let him provoke you. Except her mouth wasn't listening. 'Correction. You bought a date with me. Which means I organise it and I pick up the bill.'

'Nope. It means you get to go out with me on Sunday morning.'

She was about to protest that she couldn't, because she was working, when he added, 'And you're off duty on Sunday morning. I checked.'

She was trapped.

And maybe the fear showed in her eyes because his voice softened. 'It's only a date, Abby.'

Abby? Nobody called her that. Not even her father.

Well, *especially* not her father. He used her given

name. The one she made sure nobody at work knew about because then it would be too easy to connect her with her father. Not that she didn't love him—Keith Brydon was the most important person in the world to her. And she was incredibly proud of him. She just wanted to be seen for who she was, not dismissed as an attention-grabbing celeb's daughter riding on her famous parent's coat-tails.

Before she could protest, Lewis continued, 'We're just going somewhere and spending a bit of time together. All we're doing is getting to know each other a little. But, just so we're very clear on this, I'm not expecting you to sleep with me. Or even,' he added, 'to kiss me.'

'Right.' Oh, great. And now her voice had to croak, making it sound as if she *wanted* him to kiss her. How pathetic was that?

'Wear jeans,' he said. 'And sensible shoes.'

'Do I look like the sort of person who clip-clops around in high heels she can barely walk in?' And then she clapped a hand to her mouth. Oh, no. She hadn't actually meant to say that out loud.

His eyes crinkled at the corners. 'No. But I think you could surprise me, Abby.'

She shivered. Oh, the pictures *that* put in her head. 'I suppose now you're going to say something cheesy about finding out if I have a temper to go with my red hair.'

'It's a cliché and I wouldn't dream of it,' he said. 'Though, on this evening's showing, I think you do.'

And, damn him, his eyes were twinkling. She almost, *almost* laughed.

'You need sensible shoes,' he said again. 'Trainers would be really good. Oh, and wear your hair tied back.'

That was a given. She always wore her hair tied back. 'So what are we doing?' Despite herself, she was curious.

'You'll find out on Sunday. I'll pick you up at your place.'

She shook her head. 'There's no need. I could meet you there.'

'Ah, but you don't know where we're going.'

Irritating man. She forced herself to sound super-sweet. 'You could tell me.'

'True. But it'd be a waste of resources if we took two cars.'

'Then I'll drive.' Maybe needling him a little would make sure he agreed to it. 'Unless you're scared of letting a woman drive you?'

'No.' He laughed. 'Well, there's one exception. But she'd scare anyone.'

Ex-girlfriend? she wondered. The one that got away?

Not that it was any of her business. And not that she was interested. Because she didn't want to date Lewis Gallagher. She was only doing this because she'd made a promise to raise funds for the department.

'So are you going to make a fuss about it, or will you allow me to drive rather than direct you?'

Put like that, she didn't have much choice. She gave in. 'OK. You can drive.'

'Good. I'll pick you up at nine. Your address?'

If she didn't tell him, she was pretty sure he had the resources to find out. So she told him.

'Great. See you on Sunday.' And he was gone.

Making quite sure he had the last word, she noticed.

* * *

Abigail was really grateful for the fact that her shift on Saturday was immensely busy, with lots of people limping in with sports injuries and the like. The fact that she barely had a second to breathe also meant she didn't have to talk; the hospital grapevine had been working overtime, so everyone knew Lewis had paid a ridiculous amount of money for a date with her—and she just knew that everyone was itching to ask questions. Why would a man who could date any woman he chose pay for a date with the girl nobody wanted to go out with?

This was crazy. She wasn't his type. She wasn't a party girl or one of the women who sighed over him and thought she could reform him. And, actually, she wanted to know the real answer to that question, too. Why on earth had he paid so much money for a date with her? Was his ego really so huge that he hadn't been able to stand someone turning him down?

Though that was a bit unfair. It didn't fit in with the man she'd seen taking time to reassure a frightened child with a broken wrist earlier in the week. Or the doctor who, instead of going to get something to eat during his lunch break, had spent the time talking to the elderly man who was in for observation with stomach pains but clearly didn't have anyone to come and wait with him. Or the man who'd got a terrified yet defiant teenage girl to open up to him and tell him exactly which tablets she'd taken then had sat holding her hand and talking to her the entire way through the stomach pump that Abigail had administered.

Lewis was good with people. He gave them *time*. As a doctor, he was one of the best she'd ever worked with.

And Abigail had to admit that Lewis Gallagher was

also very easy on the eye. His dark hair was cut a bit too short for her liking, but his slate-blue eyes were beautiful. And his mouth could make her feel hot all over if she allowed herself to think about it. Not to mention the dimple in his cheek when he smiled.

But she wasn't looking for a relationship, and he was wasting his time. She'd explain; she'd give him back the money he'd paid for the date, and then hopefully that would be the end of it.

Except on Sunday he turned up at her front door with a bunch of sweet-smelling white stocks. Not a flashy, over-the-top bouquet with ribbons and cellophane and glitter, but a simple bunch of summer flowers wrapped in pretty paper. The kind of thing she'd buy herself as a treat. And it disarmed her completely.

'For you,' he said, and presented the flowers to her.

'Thank you. They're lovely.' She couldn't help breathing in their scent, enjoying it. And she'd have to put the flowers in water right now or they'd droop beyond rescue. It would be rude to leave him outside while she sorted out a vase.

But this was Lewis Gallagher. In the white shirt and formal trousers he wore with a white coat at work he looked professional and she could view him as just another colleague. In faded jeans and a black T-shirt he looked younger. Approachable. *Touchable*.

How had she ever thought she could handle this? Her social skills were rubbish. They always had been. Maybe if she hadn't grown up in an all-male environment… She pushed the thought away. This wasn't about her mother—or, rather, her lack of one. She was thirty years old and she was perfectly capable of dealing with this on her own.

'Come in,' she mumbled awkwardly.

She put the flowers in water, then buried her nose in them and breathed in the scent again. 'These are glorious.'

'I'm glad you like them,' he said.

'I wasn't expecting you to bring me flowers.'

'I believe it's official first date behaviour.'

First of three, according to the grapevine. 'So today you're on your best behaviour, next time you're going to be a bad boy, and after the third date you dump me?' She shook her head. 'No, thanks. I'll pass.'

'That's a bit unfair. You don't know me.'

True, but she wasn't going to let him guilt-trip her into agreeing to anything. 'I know your reputation.'

'Don't believe everything you hear.' He held her gaze. 'Just as I don't believe everything I hear about you, princess. Even if you are starchy and standoffish at work.'

The ice princess. Touché. 'So why *did* you place that bid?'

'Because,' he said, 'you intrigue me.'

'And because I turned you down.'

'Yes,' he admitted. 'But it's nothing to do with ego.'

'No?' she scoffed.

'No. It's because I was out of ideas on how to persuade you into joining in with the team outside work.'

So this wasn't actually a date? She found herself relaxing. 'I take it this is a team thing today, then?'

'No. It's just you and me.' He shrugged. 'And a few strangers.'

'What do you mean, strangers?'

He spread his hands and gave her a mischievous little-boy smile. 'There's only one way to find out what we're doing. Let's go.'

She wasn't that surprised to discover that his car was a convertible.

'Very flashy,' she said dryly. Though she supposed that navy blue was a tad more sophisticated than red.

'Very comfortable, actually,' he corrected her, unlocking the car and pressing a button to take the roof down.

The seats were soft, white leather. This should be clichéd and cheesy and make her want to sneer at him.

But he had a point, she discovered as she climbed in. The car *was* comfortable. And driving in the sunshine with the roof down and the wind in her hair was a real treat. She hadn't done anything like this in ages; her own car was sensible, economical and easy to park, rather than a carefree convertible.

'So where are we going?' she asked.

'About three-quarters of an hour away.'

He really wasn't going to be drawn, was he?

'Feel free to choose the music,' he said.

The first radio station she tried was dance music—not her cup of tea at all. The second was playing one of her dad's songs; she left the station playing, and couldn't help humming along to the song.

Lewis smiled at her. 'I had you pegged as listening only to highbrow stuff. Classical music. Like those tickets you bid on.'

He'd noticed that?

'See, I told you that you could surprise me.'

'So you don't like this sort of stuff?' Abigail had to remind herself not to jump to her dad's defence.

'Actually, I do. This sort of stuff is great on a play-list if you're going out for a run. But I didn't think you'd be a fan of Brydon.'

Their biggest. Not that she was going to tell Lewis that. Or why.

He didn't press her to talk, and she found herself re-laxing, enjoying the scenery.

Until he turned off the main road and she saw the sign.

'Urban Jungle Adventure Centre.' And it wasn't just the name. It was the photographs on the hoarding of what people were doing at the centre. 'We're going *zip-lining*?'

'It's one of the biggest rushes you can get.' He gave her a sidelong look as he parked the car. 'With your clothes on, that is.'

She felt the colour stain her face. 'Are you deter-mined to embarrass me?'

'No. I'm trying to make you laugh. I'm not trying to seduce you.'

'I don't understand you,' she said. 'I don't have a clue what makes you tick.'

'Snap. So let's go and have some fun finding out.'

Fun. Zip-lining. The idea of launching herself off a platform and whizzing through space, with only a flimsy harness holding her onto a line to stop her plum-meting to the ground... No, that wasn't fun. It made her palms sweat.

He frowned. 'Are you scared of heights, Abby?'

She let the diminutive pass without correcting him. 'No.'

'But you're scared of this.'

She swallowed. 'I work in the emergency department. I see accidents all the time.'

'And you think you're going to have an accident here?' His expression softened. 'It's OK, Abby. This is safe. All the staff are trained. All the equipment is tested. Very, very regularly. Your harness isn't going to break and you're not going to fall. No broken bones, no concussion, no subdural haematoma. OK?'

How had he known what the pictures were in her head? She blew out a breath. 'OK.'

'The first time you do it, I admit, it can be a bit daunting. Hardly anyone jumps off the platform on their first time. The second time, you'll know what the adrenalin rush feels like and you'll leap off as if you've never been scared.'

She doubted it. A lot. 'So this is what makes you tick. You're an adrenalin fiend.' And that was probably why he worked in the emergency department. Because it was all about speed, about split-second decisions that made the difference between life and death. Real adrenalin stuff.

'Actually, I'm probably more of an endorphin fiend,' he corrected. 'Which is why I usually go for a run before every shift, so I feel great before I start work and I'm ready to face anything.'

She'd never thought of it that way before. 'That makes sense.'

And of course he made her climb up the ladder before him. 'Ladies first.'

'You mean, you want to look at my backside,' she grumbled.

He grinned. 'That, too. It's a very nice backside.'

She gave him what she hoped was a really withering

look—no way did she want him to know just how scary she found this—and climbed up the ladder. Stubbornness got her to the top. But when it came to putting the harness on all her nerves came back. With teeth. And could she get the wretched thing on, ready for the adventure centre staff to check? Her fingers had turned into what felt like lumpy balloons.

Way to go, Abigail, she thought bitterly. How to embarrass yourself totally in front of the coolest guy in the hospital. Nothing changed, did it? She just didn't fit in.

'Let me help you,' Lewis said.

He was all ready to go, harness and wide smile both in place. Well, they *would* be, she thought crossly.

'And this isn't an excuse to touch you, by the way. Fastening the harness can be a bit tricky, and I've already gone through that learning curve.'

Now she felt like the grumpiest, most horrible person on the planet. Because Lewis was being nice, not sleazy. She'd attributed motives to him that he clearly didn't have and had thought the worst of him without any evidence to back it up. How mean was that? 'Thank you,' she muttered.

He laughed. 'That sounds more like "I want to kill you".'

'I do,' she admitted. And somehow he'd disarmed her. Somehow his smile didn't seem cocky and smug any more. He was… Shockingly, she thought, Lewis Gallagher was *nice*.

Which was dangerous. She didn't want to get close to a heartbreaker like Lewis Gallagher. She didn't want to get involved with anyone. She just wanted her nice, quiet—well, busy, she amended mentally—life as an emergency department doctor.

'OK. Step in.'

And what had seemed like an impossible web was suddenly fitting round her. Lewis's hands were brushing against her, yes, but that was only because he was checking every single buckle and every single fastening, making doubly sure that everything was done properly and she was safe. There was nothing sexual in the contact.

Which should make her feel relieved.

So why did it make her feel disappointed? Surely she wasn't so stupid as to let herself get attracted to a good-time guy like Lewis Gallagher?

'OK. Ready?' he asked.

No. Far from it. 'Yes,' she lied.

The adventure centre staff did a final check on her harness, clipped the carabiners to the zip-lines, and then she and Lewis were both standing on the very edge of the platform. Looking down over trees and a stream and—no, they didn't seriously expect her just to step off into nothingness, did they?

'You can step off or jump off,' the adventure centre guy said.

'See you at the bottom, Abby. After three,' Lewis said. 'One, two, three—whoo-hoo!'

And he jumped. He actually *jumped*.

'I hate you, Lewis Gallagher. I really, *really* hate you,' she said. Right at that moment she would've been happy to give him back the money he'd paid for their date and give double the amount to the hospital fund, as long as she didn't have to jump.

'Just step off, love. It's all right once you get going,' the adventure centre guy said. 'It's fun. Look at that ten-year-old next to you. He's enjoying it.'

So now the guy thought she was feebler than a kid? Oh, great. Her confidence dipped just a bit more.

But there was no way out of this. She had to do it.

She closed her eyes, silently cursing Lewis. Deep breath. One, two, three…

The speed shocked her into opening her eyes. It felt as if she was flying. Like a bird gliding on the air currents. Totally free, the wind rushing against her face and the sun shining.

By the time she reached the platform at the end of the zip-line, she understood exactly what Lewis had meant. This felt amazing. Like nothing she'd ever experienced.

He was there to meet her. 'OK?' he asked, his eyes filled with concern.

She blew out a breath. 'Yes.'

'Sure? You didn't look too happy when you were standing on the platform.'

'Probably because I wanted to kill you.'

'Uh-huh. And now?'

'You'll live,' she said.

He smiled, and she felt a weird sensation in her chest, as if her heart had just done a flip. Which was totally ridiculous. Number one, it wasn't physically possible and, number two, Lewis Gallagher wasn't her type. He really wasn't.

'So you enjoyed it.' He brushed her cheek gently with the backs of his fingers, and all her nerve-endings sat up and begged for more. 'Good. We get three turns. Ready for another?'

She nodded, not quite trusting her voice not to wobble and not wanting him to have any idea of how much he was affecting her.

The second time, the ladder was easier, and so was

standing on the platform This time she stepped off without hesitation.

The third time, she turned to Lewis and lifted her chin. She could do this every bit as well as he could. 'After three? One, two, three.' And she jumped, yelling, 'Whoo-hoo!'

With her customary reserve broken, Abigail Smith was beautiful, Lewis realised. Her grey eyes were shining, her cheeks were rosy with pleasure, and he suddenly desperately wanted to haul her into his arms and kiss her.

Except she was already off into space, waving her arms and striking poses as she slid down the zip-line.

If someone had told him two days ago that the ice princess of the hospital would let herself go and enjoy herself this much, he would've scoffed. He'd brought her here as much to rattle her as anything else.

But he'd been hoist with his own petard, because she didn't seem rattled at all.

Unlike him. Abigail Smith had managed to rattle him, big time.

He jumped off the platform and followed her down; he was far enough behind for her to be already taking off the safety harness when he reached the landing platform.

'So are you going to admit it?' he asked when he'd removed his own harness and handed it to the assistant at the bottom of the zip-line.

'What?'

'That you enjoyed it.'

She nodded. 'If you'd told me earlier that this was where we were going, I would've made an excuse. I would've paid back your money and given the same amount to the hospital, so nobody lost out.'

'But you would've lost out.' He held her gaze. 'And I don't mean just the money.'

'Yes. You're right.'

He liked the fact that she could admit it when she was wrong. 'That's why I didn't tell you.'

'Thank you for bringing me here. I never would've thought I'd enjoy something like this. But—yes, it was fun.'

Oh, help. She had *dimples* when she smiled. Who would've thought that the serious, keep-herself-to-herself doctor would be this gorgeous when her reserve was down? He hadn't expected her to be anything like this. And he was horribly aware that Abigail Smith could really get under his skin.

'Let's go exploring,' he said. He needed to move, distract himself from her before he said something stupid. Or did something worse—like giving in to the temptation to lean over and kiss her.

CHAPTER TWO

ABIGAIL AND LEWIS spent the next couple of hours exploring every activity at the centre, including the almost vertical slides and the climbing wall. Abigail didn't even seem to mind when they got a bit wet on the water chute, though Lewis's pulse spiked as he imagined how she'd look with her skin still damp from showering with him.

'Penny for them?' she asked.

No way. If he told her, she'd either slap his face or go silent on him, and he wanted to get to know more of this playful side of her. 'Time for lunch,' he said instead.

'Only on condition you let me pay. Because you've paid for everything else today.'

'And you don't like being beholden.'

'Exactly.'

Someone had hurt her, he thought. Broken her trust. Maybe that was why she kept herself to herself so much: to protect herself from being hurt again. 'Then thank you. I would love you to buy me lunch.'

She looked faintly surprised, as if she'd expected him to argue, and then looked relieved.

'There really aren't any strings to today, Abby,' he said softly. 'This is all about having fun.'

'And I am having fun.'

Although her smile was a little bit too bright. What was she hiding?

There was no point in asking; he knew she didn't trust him enough to tell him and she'd make up some anodyne excuse or change the subject. So he simply smiled back and led her to the cafeteria.

'What would you like?' she asked.

He glanced at the board behind the counter. 'A burger, chips and a cola, please.'

'Junk food. Tut. And you a health professional,' she teased.

'Hey, I'm burning every bit of it off,' he protested.

She smiled. 'Go and find us a table and I'll queue up.'

When she joined him at the table with a tray of food, Lewis noticed that she'd chosen a jacket potato with salad and cottage cheese, and a bottle of mineral water. 'Super-healthy. Now I feel guilty for eating junk.'

She looked anxious. 'I was only teasing you.'

'Yeah. I was teasing, too.' He gave her a reassuring smile. 'Thank you. That looks good.'

He kept the conversation light during lunch, and then they went back to exploring the park.

'Do you want to do the zip-line again?' he asked.

'Can we?'

'Sure.'

And, as well as his usual adrenalin rush, Lewis got an extra kick from the fact that she was so clearly enjoying something they'd both thought was well outside her comfort zone.

'Thank you. I've had a really nice time,' she said when they got back to his car.

'The date's not over yet.'

She blinked. 'Isn't it?'

'I thought we could have dinner,' he said.

She looked down at her jeans and her T-shirt. 'I'm not really dressed for dinner.'

'You're fine as you are. I don't have a dress code.'

She frowned. 'I'm sorry, I'm not quite with you.'

'I'm cooking for us. At my place,' he explained.

This time, she laughed. '*You're* cooking?'

He shrugged. 'I can cook.'

She smiled. 'I bet you only learned to impress your girlfriends at university.'

No. He'd learned because he'd had to, when he'd been fourteen. Because the only way he and his little sisters would've had anything to eat had been if he'd cooked it. Not that he had any intention of telling Abigail about that. 'Something like that,' he said lightly, and drove them back to his flat.

'Can we stop at an off-licence or something so I can get a bottle of wine as my contribution to dinner?' she asked on the way.

'There's no need. I have wine.'

'But I haven't contributed anything.'

'You have. You bought me lunch.'

'This was supposed to be my date,' she reminded him.

'Tough. I hijacked it, and we're on my rules now,' he said with a smile. 'Just chill, and we'll have dinner.'

Something smelled good, Abigail thought when Lewis let her inside his flat. Clearly he'd planned this, and it wasn't the frozen pizza she'd been half expecting him to produce for dinner.

'It'll take five minutes for me to sort the vegetables.

The bathroom's through there if you need it,' he said, indicating a door.

She washed her hands and splashed a little water on her face, then stared at herself in the mirror. She looked a total mess and her hair was all over the place, despite the fact she'd tied it back, and she didn't have a comb with her so it'd just have to stay looking like a bird's nest. Then again, this wasn't a *date* date so it really didn't matter how she looked, did it?

When she emerged from the bathroom, she could hear the clatter of crockery in the kitchen. 'Is there anything I can do to help?' she called.

'No, just take a seat,' he called back.

There was a bistro table in the living room with two chairs. The table was set nicely; he'd clearly made an effort.

There was an array of photographs on the mantelpiece, and she couldn't resist going over for a closer look. At first glance, Abigail wasn't surprised that most of them seemed to involve Lewis with his arm round someone female. One of them showed him holding a baby in a white christening gown.

His baby? Surely not. If Lewis had a child, he would've mentioned it.

But then she saw a wedding photograph with three women and Lewis. When she studied it, she could see the family likenesses: the bridesmaids were clearly the bride's sisters. And the same women were in all the photographs. One of them had the same eyes as Lewis; one had his smile; all had his dark hair.

Which meant they had to be Lewis's sisters. She guessed that the baby belonged to one of them, and Lewis was a doting uncle-cum-godfather.

He came through to the living room, carrying two plates. 'OK?' he asked.

'Just admiring your photographs—your sisters, I presume?'

'And my niece.' He nodded. 'My best girls.'

She'd already worked out that he was close to his family. What would it be like to have a sibling who'd always be there for you, someone you could ring at stupid o'clock in the morning when the doubts hit and you wondered what the hell you were doing? Being an only child, she'd got used to dealing with everything on her own.

'They look nice,' she offered.

'They are. Most of the time. You know what it's like.'

No, she didn't. 'Yes,' she fibbed.

'Come and sit down.'

He put the plate down in front of her, and she felt her eyes widen. Oh, no. She should've said something. Right back when he'd first told her they were having dinner here. But she'd simply assumed that by 'cooking' he'd meant just throwing a frozen cheese and tomato pizza into the oven, and then she'd been distracted by the photographs.

Dinner was presented beautifully, right down to the garnish of chopped fresh herbs.

But no way could she eat it.

Maybe if she ate just the inside of the jacket potato, then hid the chicken stew under the skin?

He clearly noticed her hesitation. 'Oh, hell. I didn't think to ask. And, given what you had for lunch…' He frowned, and she could see the second he made the connection. 'You're vegetarian, aren't you?'

'Yes.' She swallowed hard. 'But don't worry about

it. You've gone to so much trouble. If you don't mind, I'll just eat the jacket potato and the veg.'

'A casserole isn't much trouble. And I'm not going to make you pick at your food. Give me ten minutes.' Before she had a chance to protest, he'd whisked her plate away.

She followed him into the kitchen. 'Lewis, really—you don't have to go to any more trouble. Honestly. It's my fault. I should've said something before. Leave it. I'll just get a taxi home.'

'You will *not*,' he said crisply. 'I promised you dinner, and dinner you shall have. Are you OK with pasta?'

'I…'

'Yes or no, Abby?' His tone was absolutely implacable.

And, after all the adrenalin of their day at the adventure centre, she was hungry. She gave in. 'Yes.'

'And spinach?'

'Yes.'

'Good. I know you're OK with dairy, or you wouldn't have eaten cottage cheese. But I've already made enough wrong assumptions today, so I'm going to check. Are you OK with garlic and mascarpone?'

'Love them,' she said, squirming and feeling as if she was making a total fuss.

'Good. Dinner will be ten minutes. Go and pour yourself a glass of wine.' He was already heating oil in a pan, then squashed a clove of garlic and chopped an onion faster than she'd ever seen it done before.

So much for thinking he'd exaggerated his cooking skills. Lewis Gallagher actually knew his way around a kitchen. And he hadn't been trying to impress her—he was trying to be hospitable. Bossing her around in exactly the way he probably bossed his kid sisters around.

She went back into his living room, poured herself a glass of wine and then poured a second glass for him before returning to the kitchen with the glasses. 'I, um, thought you might like this.'

'Thank you. I would.' He smiled at her.

The spinach was wilting into the onions and the kettle was boiling, ready for the pasta. 'Sorry, I'm out of flour, or I'd make us some flatbread to go with it.'

And she'd just bet he made his bread by hand, not with a machine. Lewis Gallagher was turning out to be so much more domesticated than she'd thought. And the fact he'd noticed that she couldn't eat the food and guessed why... There was more to him than just the shallow party boy. Much more.

Which made him dangerous to her peace of mind.

She should back away, right now.

But then he started talking to her about food and bread, putting her at her ease, and she found herself relaxing with him. Ten minutes later, she carried her own plate through to the living room: pasta with a simple garlic, spinach and mascarpone sauce.

'This is really good,' she said after the first mouthful. 'Thank you.'

He inclined his head. 'I'm only sorry that I didn't ask you earlier if you were veggie. Dani would have my hide for that.'

'Dani?'

'The oldest of my girls. She's vegetarian.'

Which explained why he'd been able to whip up something without a fuss. And not pasta with the usual jar of tomato sauce with a handful of grated cheese dumped onto it, which in her experience most people seemed to think passed for good vegetarian food.

'So your sisters are all younger than you?' she asked.

He nodded. 'Dani's an actuary, Manda's a drama teacher, and Ronnie—short for Veronica—is a librarian.'

'Do they all live in London?'

'Dani does. Ronnie's in Manchester and Manda's in Cambridge. Which I guess is near enough to London for me to see her and Louise reasonably often.'

'Louise being the baby?' she guessed.

'My niece. Goddaughter.' He grinned. 'Manda named her after me, though I hope Louise is a bit better behaved than I am when she grows up.'

Abigail smiled back at him. 'Since you're the oldest, I'm surprised none of them were tempted to follow you into medicine.'

It wasn't that surprising. Lewis had been the one to follow *them* to university. Because how could he have just gone off at eighteen to follow his own dreams, leaving the girls to deal with their mother and fend for themselves? So he'd stayed. He'd waited until Ronnie was eighteen and ready to fly the nest, before applying to read medicine and explaining at the interview why his so-called gap year had actually lasted for six.

'No,' he said lightly. 'What about you? Brothers or sisters?'

She looked away. 'Neither. Just me.'

'That explains the ice princess. Daddy's girl,' he said.

Daddy's girl.

Did he *know*?

Had he made the connection with 'Cinnamon Baby',

the little girl with ringlets who'd been the paparazzi's darling, smiling for the cameras on her father's shoulders? She really hoped not. Abigail didn't use her first name any more, and it had been years since the paparazzi had followed her about. Even so, the times when her identity had been leaked in the past had made her paranoid about it happening again.

And there was no guile in Lewis's face. Abigail had already leaped to a few wrong conclusions about him, and she knew she wasn't being fair to him.

'I suppose I am, a bit,' she said.

'Is your dad a doctor?' he asked.

'No. What about your parents?'

He shook his head, and for a moment she was sure she saw sadness in his eyes, though when she blinked it had gone. Maybe she'd imagined it.

Pudding turned out to be strawberries and very posh vanilla ice cream.

'Do I take it you make your own ice cream?' Abigail asked.

Lewis laughed. 'No. There's an Italian deli around the corner that sells the nicest ice cream in the world, so there's no need to make my own—though I would love an ice-cream maker.' He rolled his eyes. 'But my girls say I already have far too many gadgets.'

'Boys and their toys,' she said lightly.

'Cooking relaxes me.' He grinned. 'But I admit I like gadgets as well. As long as they're useful, otherwise they're just clutter and a waste of space.'

Abigaïl glanced at her watch and was surprised to discover how late it was. 'I'd better get that taxi.'

'Absolutely not. I'm driving you home. And I only had one glass of wine, so I'm under the limit.'

It was easier not to protest. Though, with the roof up, his car seemed much more intimate. Just the two of them in an enclosed space.

He insisted on seeing her to her door.

'Would you like to come in for coffee?' she asked.

He shook his head. 'You're on an early shift tomorrow, so it wouldn't be fair. But thank you for the offer.'

'Thank you for today, Lewis. I really enjoyed it.'

'Me, too,' he said.

And this was where she unlocked the door, closed it behind her and ended everything.

Except her mouth had other ideas.

'Um, those concert tickets I bid for at the fundraiser. It's on Friday night. It probably isn't your thing, but if you'd like to, um, go with me, you're very welcome.'

He looked at her and gave her a slow smile that made her toes curl. 'Thank you. I'd like that very much.'

'Not as a date,' she added hastily, 'just because I have a spare ticket.' She didn't want him thinking she was chasing him. Because she wasn't.

Was she?

Right at that moment, she didn't have a clue what she was doing. Lewis Gallagher rattled her composure, big time. And, if she was honest with herself, she'd been lonely since she'd started her new job. Lewis was the first of her colleagues who'd really made an effort with her, and part of her wanted to make the effort back.

'As friends,' he said. 'That works for me. See you tomorrow, Abby.' He touched her cheek briefly with the backs of his fingers. 'Sleep well.'

Despite the fresh air and the exercise, Abigail didn't

think she would—because her skin was tingling where Lewis had touched her. And the knowledge that he could affect her like that totally threw her. 'You, too. Goodnight,' she mumbled, and fled into the safety of her flat.

CHAPTER THREE

'JUST THE PERSON I wanted to see.' Marina Fenton smiled at Abigail. 'Are you free for lunch today?'

It was the last thing Abigail had expected. She normally had lunch on her own and hid behind a journal so nobody joined her or started a conversation with her. 'I, um...' Oh, help. Why was she so socially awkward? She was fine with her dad's crowd; then again, they'd known her for her entire life. It was just new people she wasn't so good with. And, growing up in an all-male environment, she'd never quite learned the knack of making friends with women. She didn't have a clue about girl talk. 'Well, patients permitting, I guess so,' she said cautiously.

'Good. I'll see you in the kitchen at twelve, and we can walk to the canteen together.'

'OK.' Feeling a bit like a rabbit in the headlights, Abigail took refuge in the triage notes for her next patient.

At twelve, she headed for the staff kitchen. Marina was waiting for her there, as promised, but so was Sydney Ranieri, which Abigail hadn't expected.

'I know I'm officially off duty today, but Marina said she was having lunch with you and I thought it'd

be nice to join you both—if you don't mind, that is?'
Sydney asked.

'I, um—no, of course not.' But it threw her. Why
would the two other doctors want to have lunch with
her?

'By the way, lunch is on us,' Marina said, ushering
her out of the department and towards the hospital canteen. 'Because we've been feeling immensely guilty
about the weekend.'

Oh. So that was what this was all about. Guilt. Well,
she'd never been much good at making friends. Stupid
to think that might change with a different hospital. Abigail shook her head. 'There's no need, on either count.
I was happy to help with the fundraising. There's nothing to feel guilty about.'

'So it went well, then, your date with Lewis?' Sydney asked.

Yes and no. Except it hadn't really been a date. And
it wouldn't be fair to Lewis to discuss it. 'It was OK.'

'OK?' Sydney and Marina shared a glance. 'Women
never say that about a date with Lewis.'

Abigail spread her hands. 'He took me zip-lining.'

'Ah.' There was a wealth of understanding in Sydney's voice. 'That's the thing about the male doctors in
this department. They all seem to like doing mad things.
Marina's husband organised a sponsored abseil down
the hospital tower. All two hundred and fifty feet of it.'
She shuddered. 'And somehow he persuaded the whole
department into doing it.'

'Mmm, I can imagine that,' Abigail said dryly. Max
had persuaded her to do something well outside her
comfort zone, too.

'But it had its good points. I met Marco because I got

stuck,' Sydney said. 'Faced with the reality of walking backwards into nothing, I just froze.' She grimaced. 'Marco sang me down.'

'He sang you down?' Abigail couldn't help being intrigued. 'How?'

'He got me to sing with him, to distract me from the fact that I was on the edge of this huge tower, and then he talked me through every step. I was still shaking at the bottom of the tower when he abseiled down next to me.' Sydney rolled her eyes. 'And when he landed, it was as if he'd done nothing scarier than walking along the pavement towards me.'

'That sounds exactly like the sort of thing Lewis would do,' Abigail said.

'He wasn't with the department then, or he probably would have done.' Marina smiled, but her eyes held a trace of anxiety. 'Was it really that awful?'

'The first time I had to step off that platform, with nothing but a bit of webbing and a rope between me and a huge drop, I wanted to kill him,' Abigail admitted, and they all laughed. 'But then—once I'd actually done it, it was fun. The second time round was a lot better.'

'Good.' Marina rested her hand briefly on Abigail's arm. 'I've been feeling terrible all weekend, thinking that we pushed you into offering that date. I had no idea that Lewis was going to bid for you.'

'Neither did I,' Abigail said dryly.

'He's a nice guy,' Sydney said. 'As a colleague, he's totally reliable at work and he's good company on team nights out. But, um, maybe I should warn you that when it comes to his personal life, he doesn't do commitment.'

'Three dates and you're out. So I heard,' Abigail said. Though she knew that Lewis *did* do commitment, at least where his family was concerned. He was really close to his sisters and his niece. Though, now she thought of it, he hadn't had any pictures of his parents on display in his flat. Which was odd.

And why would someone who was close to his family be so wary of risking his heart? Had someone broken it, years ago?

Though it was none of her business.

They were just colleagues. Possibly starting to become friends. Though she wasn't going to tell Marina and Sydney that they were going to the concert together later in the week. She didn't want them to get the wrong idea.

Once they'd queued up at the counter and bought their lunch, they found a quiet table in the canteen.

'So are you going to see Lewis again?' Marina asked.

'Considering that we work in the same department, I'd say there's a good chance of seeing him in Resus or what have you, depending on the roster,' Abigail said lightly.

'That isn't what I meant.'

Abigail smiled. 'I know. But we're colleagues, Marina. He only bid for that date because—well, he said he was trying to persuade me to do more things with the team.'

'Helping you settle in. Fixing things.' Sydney looked thoughtful. 'Actually, Lewis is like that. He sees something that maybe could work better if it was done differently, and he fixes it.' She smiled. 'Well, I guess that's why we all chose this career. We're fixers.'

'Definitely,' Abigail said, and was relieved when the discussion turned away from Lewis. By the end of the lunch break she found herself really enjoying the company of the other two doctors. They weren't like the mean girls who'd made her life a misery at school. They were *nice*.

'I'd better get back,' she said when she'd finished her coffee.

'Me, too,' Marina said. She winked at Sydney. 'It's all right for you part-timers.'

Sydney just laughed. 'It's fun being a lady who lunches. Well, at least part time. I'd never give up work totally because I'd miss it too much. I've enjoyed today. Let's make it a regular thing,' she suggested. 'I work Tuesdays, Wednesdays and Thursdays. Which of those days is best for you, Abby?'

The same diminutive Lewis had used. Something that had never happened in previous hospitals—she'd always been Dr Smith or Abigail. But here at the London Victoria it was different. There was much more of a sense of the department members being a team. Being friends outside work. And Marina and Sydney were offering her precisely that: friendship. For her own sake, rather than because she was Keith Brydon's daughter—as people had in the past whenever her identity had leaked out.

For once in her life Abigail was actually fitting in. It felt weird; but it felt *good*. And she didn't want that feeling to stop.

'How about Wednesdays?' Abigail asked.

'Excellent. Wednesday at twelve it is, patients permitting—and if one of us is held up, the others will save a space at the table,' Marina said with a smile. 'It's a date.'

Abigail didn't see Lewis all day, even in passing. She'd been rostered in Minors for her shift and according to the departmental whiteboard he was in Resus. She wasn't sure if she was more relieved that she didn't have to face him or disappointed that she hadn't seen him. And it annoyed her that she felt so mixed up about the situation. She'd worked hard and she'd been happy to make the sacrifices in her personal life to get where she wanted to be in her professional life. So why, why, why was she even thinking about dating a man who had commitment issues and wasn't her type?

She was still brooding about it the next day. Though then it started to get busy in the department.

She picked up her next set of triage notes. Headache and temperature. Normally patients with a simple virus would be treated by the triage nurse and sent home with painkillers and advice. But this wasn't just a simple case, from the look of the notes: the nurse had written *'Query opiates'* at the bottom of the page. So the headache and temperature could be part of a reaction to whatever drug the patient had taken.

'Eddie McRae?' she called.

An ashen-faced man walked up the corridor, supported by another man.

She introduced herself swiftly. 'So you have a headache and temperature, Mr McRae?'

'Eddie,' he muttered. 'I feel terrible.'

'Have you been in contact with anyone who has a virus?' she asked.

'I don't think so.'

So it could be withdrawal or a bad reaction to the drugs he'd taken. His breathing was fast, she noticed. 'Can I take your pulse?'

'Sure.'

His pulse was also fast, so Eddie could well be suffering from sepsis.

'Have you taken anything?' she asked gently.

This time Eddie didn't say a word, and she had a pretty good idea why. 'I'm not going to lecture you or call the police,' she reassured him. 'My job's to help you feel better than you do right now. And the more information you give me, the easier it's going to be for me to get it right first time.'

'He took something Saturday night,' his friend said. 'He's been ill today, with a headache and temperature.'

'So it could be a reaction to what you took. Did you swallow it?'

Eddie shook his head and grimaced in pain.

'Injected?' At his slight nod, she said, 'Can I see where?'

He shrugged off his cardigan. There were track marks on his arm, as she'd expected, but the redness and swelling definitely weren't what she'd expected.

'Eddie, I really need to know what you took,' she said gently.

'Heroin,' his friend said.

'OK.' She knew that the withdrawal symptoms from heroin usually peaked forty-eight to seventy-two hours after the last dose, but this didn't seem like the withdrawal cases she'd seen in the past.

'Are you sleeping OK, Eddie?' she asked.

'Yeah.'

'Do you have any pain, other than your head?'

He nodded. 'My stomach.'

'Have you been sick or had diarrhoea?'

He grimaced. 'No.'

Abigail had a funny feeling about this. Although she

hadn't actually seen a case at her last hospital, there had been a departmental circular about heroin users suffering from anthrax after using contaminated supplies, and an alarm bell was ringing at the back of her head. There was no sign of black eschar, the dead tissue cast off from the surface of the skin, which was one of the big giveaways with anthrax, but she had a really strong feeling about this. Right now she could do with some advice from a more senior colleague.

'I'm going to leave you in here for a second, if that's OK,' she said. 'I have a hunch I know what's wrong, but there's something I want to check with a colleague, and then I think we'll be able to do something to help you.'

'Just make the pain stop. Please,' Eddie said.

She stepped out of the cubicle and pulled the curtain closed behind her. With any luck Max or Marco would be free—in this case, she needed a second opinion from a consultant.

But the first person she saw was Lewis.

'OK, Abby?' he asked. 'You look a bit worried.'

'I need a second opinion on a patient. Is Max or Marco around?'

'Marco's in Resus and Max is in a meeting,' he said. 'Will I do?'

Although they were officially the same grade, she knew that Lewis was older than her—which made him more experienced, her senior colleague. And really she should've asked him instead of trying to track down Max or Marco. She grimaced. 'Sorry, I didn't mean to imply that you weren't good eno—'

'Relax, Abby,' he cut in. 'I didn't think you were saying that at all. What's the problem?'

'My patient took heroin on Saturday. He has a headache and a temperature, and what looks like soft tissue sepsis—not the normal sort of reaction at the injection site. At my last hospital, we had case notes about anthrax in heroin users. Do you know if there's anything like that happening in this area?'

'No—but you know as well as I do that if something affects one area of the city, it's going to spread to the rest, so it's only a matter of time. You think this is anthrax?'

'There's no sign of black eschar. I don't have any proof. Just a gut feeling that this is more than just withdrawal symptoms or a bad reaction.'

'I'd run with it. Do you want me to take a look to back you up? And if it is anthrax, we can split the notifications between us and save a bit of time.'

Anthrax was a notifiable disease, and the lab would also need to know of her suspicions when she sent any samples through for testing so they could take extra precautions. 'Thanks, that would be good,' she said gratefully.

Lewis walked back to the cubicle with her and she introduced him to Eddie McRae. Lewis examined him swiftly and looked at her. 'I think you're right,' he said quietly.

Abigail took a deep breath. 'I'll need to do a couple more tests to check, Eddie, but I think you have anthrax.'

'But—how? We're not terrorists or anything!' Eddie looked shocked. 'We've never had anything to do with that sort of stuff. How can I have anthrax?'

'Anthrax is a bacterium,' she explained. 'It can survive as spores in soil for years. It's not that common now in the UK, but somehow anthrax has found its way into the heroin supply chain so the drugs have been contaminated. There have been a few cases of heroin users with anthrax in mainland Europe and Scotland— and parts of London, too, because we had some in my last hospital.'

'My granddad was a farmer. His cattle got anthrax years ago and they all had to be killed. Is Eddie going to die?' Eddie's friend asked, looking anxious.

'It's treatable,' Lewis reassured him. 'We can give you broad-spectrum antibiotics to deal with the infection, but you'll also need surgery, Eddie.'

'Surgery?' Eddie looked panicky.

'The area where you injected the heroin is swollen and red, which tells me it's infected,' Abigail explained. 'This is where the anthrax spores are concentrated. If we take away the dead tissue, then that takes away the toxins and they won't spread any further into your system.'

Eddie shook his head. 'I can't lose my arm, I just can't. How can I play the guitar without my arm?'

Abigail sighed inwardly. That had happened to someone her dad knew: the young guitarist hadn't been able to cope with the amputation after the car accident and had finally taken an overdose.

'You're not going to lose your arm, Eddie. I promise. All I'm going to do is take away the damaged tissues.'

'It's going to hurt.'

'I'll give you local anaesthetic so you won't feel it, though I will be honest and admit you'll feel a bit sore afterwards.'

Eddie shook his head, wide-eyed in fear. 'I don't want you to do it.'

'If we don't take away the infected tissue,' Lewis

said softly, 'the antibiotics won't be enough to deal with the anthrax. Some of those cases Dr Smith was talking about were fatal because they didn't come to the hospital in time for treatment. You've got a really good chance of getting over it right now. Plus, if you leave it, it'll hurt more.'

'I really won't feel it when you...' Eddie gulped '...use the knife?'

'You really won't,' Lewis reassured him.

Eddie swallowed hard. 'OK. I'll do it.'

Lewis patted his shoulder. 'Good for you, Eddie.'

Making sure she was using gloves, a gown and a mask, Abigail took a blood sample. With all the track marks on Eddie's arms, it was hard to find a good spot to take a sample, but she managed it. She labelled the sample as high risk, and did the same with the samples of tissue and sputum.

'Do you want me to talk to the public health lot while you talk to the lab?' Lewis asked.

'Thanks. That'd be good,' she said gratefully.

The admin side seemed to take for ever, but finally Abigail was back with Lewis in Eddie's cubicle. 'Once we've sorted out your arm, I'm going to put you on a drip with antibiotics,' she said to Eddie. 'The blood test will show if I need to put you on a different sort of antibiotics.'

He nodded, and looked anxiously at his friend. 'Is it catching? Could Mike here have anthrax because of me?'

'It doesn't spread from person to person by air droplets like a cold does, if that's what you're asking,' Lewis said. He looked at Mike. 'But if you have a tiny cut on your skin and infected body fluids get in, then it's a possibility. We can do a blood test on you now to check.'

Mike blew out a breath. 'Thanks. I don't feel ill, not like Eddie does.'

'Better to be safe,' Abigail said. 'The thing is, if you've got infected blood or sputum on your clothes, washing won't be enough to kill the spores. So I'm going to have to put you in a hospital gown, Eddie, and destroy your clothes. And you're going to be in the ward overnight so we can keep an eye on you and keep those antibiotics going.' She looked at Mike. 'Can you make sure that everyone you know is aware there's a problem with anthrax and the symptoms to look out for?'

'Yeah, I will.' Mike stared at the floor. 'I thought you'd have a go at us about taking drugs in the first place.'

'Take the lecture as read,' she said dryly. 'It's your choice and not my business, but right now you need to know there are extra risks in those choices because the supply's been contaminated.'

'I guess this is a wake-up call,' Eddie said.

'We can help you,' Abigail said. 'All you have to do is ask, and we will help you.' She sorted out a gown for Eddie and a bag for his contaminated clothes, and waited for him to change before going back into the cubicle. 'OK. Are you ready now for me to sort out your arm?'

'No, but I guess I don't have a choice. Can Mike stay?'

'Sure.' She smiled at Mike. 'Are you OK with the sight of blood? Because if you're not, just keep looking at Eddie's face and not at what Lewis and I are doing. And if you feel faint, stick your head between your knees.'

'Got it.' Mike blew out a breath. 'I think this might be a wake-up call for me as well.'

Between them, Abigail and Lewis administered the local anaesthetic and reassurance to Eddie, and she began to remove the damaged tissue.

Although Lewis had worked with Abigail before, it was the first time he'd seen her do a surgical debridement, and he was impressed. She was very neat, very quick, and she put both Eddie and Mike at their ease.

'Nice work,' he said when they left cubicles.

'Thanks. Though it wasn't just mine.' She smiled at him. 'You're the one who talked Eddie into letting me give him the proper treatment.'

'Pleasure. Shall we grab a coffee? I need to debrief you on what the health prevention agency and the hospital infection control team said.'

'Sounds good to me,' she said.

On Wednesday, the results proved that Eddie did indeed have anthrax. Abigail managed to find Lewis in the department. 'We were right. It was anthrax.'

'You were the one who noticed,' he said. 'Good call.'

'Thanks.' Funny how his praise made her feel as if she was glowing inside.

And that glow lasted during her lunch with Sydney and Marina.

'There's a team bowling evening on Friday. It was booked last month, and Jay's had to drop out, so if you want to come and make up the team it'd be good to have you,' Marina said.

No pressure, just an invite from someone who was becoming her friend. Abigail was about to say yes when she thought about the date. 'Friday? Sorry, I would've come, but I bid on tickets for a concert at the fundraiser, and the performance is on Friday.' Not that she was going to admit who she was going with.

But she didn't want to just leave it there. To be stand-offish, the way she'd always been. She needed to make an effort. Taking a risk, she added, 'But if you have a space next time, I'll be there. Even though I'm not that good at bowling.'

'It's not the result that matters—it's whether we have fun. The next department night out is going to be ice skating,' Sydney said.

'I've never done that,' Abigail said.

Another brush-off? No. She was going to make this work. She hoped that her smile didn't betray how awkward she felt. 'But I'll give it a go if there's space for me.'

'Oh, there's space. Way to go, Abby,' Sydney said, smiling at her and holding her palm up in a high-five gesture.

Still feeling that warm glow, Abigail high-fived her. If someone had told her three months ago that her life would change totally at the London Victoria, she would've scoffed. But here life was different.

Life was good.

CHAPTER FOUR

ABIGAIL HAD A day off on Friday. Lewis was working, but he'd arranged to meet her at her flat before the concert. She couldn't settle all day, and spent ages choosing what to wear. Which was ridiculous, because she'd already made it very clear to him that this wasn't a date. And, besides, Lewis wouldn't care in the slightest what she was wearing.

Half of her didn't want him to notice that she'd made an effort. The other half was longing for him to tell her she looked nice. And that made her really cross with herself. She was an independent woman, not a needy child. She didn't need someone to tell her what she looked like.

Crossly, she changed her outfit for the third time. And this time she made sure that her shoes were flat and sensible, and she kept her hair tied back instead of wearing it loose.

She tried doing a cryptic crossword to keep herself from looking at the clock to see how long she'd have to wait for Lewis to meet her. It worked; but when she'd finished she glanced at her watch and realised that he was late.

Or was he? Had he changed his mind, and he just

wasn't going to turn up? Or maybe he'd had a better offer and he'd make some charming excuse the next time he saw her.

Just when she was really stewing in misery, her phone beeped to signal a text message. She glanced at the screen. Lewis. She flicked into the message.

Sorry, tricky patient. Running a bit late. Meet you in foyer of concert hall instead? Sorry. L.

Working in medicine wasn't like an office job. You couldn't just tell your patient to go away and come back tomorrow, and she would've thought less of Lewis if he'd handed over his patient to someone else to deal with rather than seeing things through.

OK, see you there, she texted back.

She checked that she'd put the tickets in her handbag, headed for the concert hall and bought two programmes. She waited for Lewis in the foyer, glancing up from the programme every few seconds in case he was walking through the door. But nothing. It was getting to the point where she thought he wasn't going to make it in time when he rushed in.

'Sorry. After all that there was a delay on the Tube as well—and either your phone's switched off or you don't have a signal in here, because I did try to ring you from the station.'

'Technology, eh?' she said lightly. 'Never mind. You're here now. Let's go in. I bought you a programme.'

'Thanks.' He kissed her swiftly on the cheek.

And it was totally ridiculous that her skin tingled where his lips had touched her.

They made it to their seats by the skin of their teeth. Lewis glanced at the programme. 'Oh, excellent. I love Beethoven.'

Abigail looked at him, faintly surprised. She'd expected him only to like the kind of pop the radio had been playing in his car. 'Beethoven's my favourite, too.' Maybe they had more in common than she'd first thought.

Two minutes after the orchestra began playing she was lost in the magic of the music. And then, during the slow movement of Beethoven's *Pathétique* sonata—a piece of music she'd always loved—Lewis reached over to hold her hand.

He didn't look at her and she didn't look at him, but it felt right to curl her fingers round his. And to let him hold her hand throughout the rest of the concert.

At the end, he loosened his hand from hers and Abigail could see in his expression that he was as surprised by what he'd just done as she was.

She could pretend it hadn't happened, retreat back into her shell and be safe.

Or she could take a risk.

At that moment, it felt as if she was at a crossroads. Which way was the right way to go?

And why was she even thinking about this anyway? She wasn't looking for a relationship. Especially with a guy who had a three-dates-and-you're-out rule.

But they'd gone to the concert together. Dinner wouldn't hurt, would it? 'Have you eaten yet?' she asked.

He shook his head. 'I didn't have time.'

Risk. She could take a risk.

'We could, um, go and get something now, if you like,' she suggested diffidently.

His eyes crinkled at the corners. 'Are you asking me out, Dr Smith?'

Panic flooded through her. Oh, help. What did she do now? 'I...um... Just as—' she began.

'A friend,' he finished, 'who realises that I've had a really long day and am absolutely starving. That would be good.'

She wasn't quite sure if he'd been teasing her about asking him out or if he'd been serious under that jokey exterior. She definitely wasn't going to be gauche enough to ask. 'Shall we go to the first place we see?' she asked.

He laughed. 'I can't see you doing a greasy spoon place.'

'If they did good eggs, I'd be OK. But you have a point. I'd rather not go to a burger bar, if you don't mind.'

Just around the corner from the concert hall there was an Italian restaurant. 'Is this OK for you?' she asked.

'Lovely.'

Once they were seated at the table, Lewis studied the menu, looking serious.

'You don't have to choose something vegetarian on my account,' she said.

He raised an eyebrow at her. 'Are you sure? I mean, it was different before I knew you were vegetarian. I don't eat meat if I go out with Dani.'

'I'm sure. I'd rather not eat meat, but I don't think that everyone else has to give it up for me—forcing my choices on someone else feels wrong. Pick what you want.'

His smile made her feel warm inside. 'Thank you.'

Abigail ordered gnocchi with sage butter and portion of garlicky spinach; Lewis ordered lasagne.

'I'm afraid this is my big weakness,' he said with a grin. 'It's my absolutely favourite comfort food—and I've had the kind of day that makes me really need it.'

'Uh-huh.' She tried not to be disappointed that her company and the music hadn't been enough to make it better.

'Except,' he said softly, 'this evening with you. That was food for the soul and made me feel a hell of a lot better.'

Was he only saying it because her disappointment had shown in her face and he was being charming?

The question must've been obvious because he said, 'I guess I'm just greedy. My favourite food and good company—that's the best way to spend a Friday night.'

They'd also ordered bread and olives to keep them going until the main course was ready, and their fingers brushed against each other as they reached for the bread at the same time. Abigail was horribly aware of his nearness, of the feel of his skin against hers—and of the possibilities blooming in her head.

'You first,' he said softly.

She hardly dared look at him as she took some bread. And she was furious when she spilled some of the oil on the table. So now he'd know that she was rattled. Not good. Luckily the napkin was paper and not linen, so she dabbed at the puddle of oil with it.

'Let me help,' he said, and cleaned up with remarkable speed and efficiency.

And now she felt hopeless as well as gauche.

'Abby,' he said softly.

She had no choice but to look at him.

'Thank you for taking me to the concert,' he said.

'My pleasure,' she mumbled. 'I had a spare ticket

and it would've been a waste not to use it.' Which was only part of the truth. She'd wanted to spend time with Lewis. And that scared her.

'You've gone shy on me.' He frowned slightly. 'I thought we were becoming friends?'

She wasn't sure *what* they were becoming. And it worried her that she was starting to feel things about Lewis Gallagher that really weren't sensible.

She took refuge in asking about work. 'So what happened with your tricky patient?'

He grimaced. 'He came in because he'd blacked out at work and one of his colleagues called the ambulance. I noticed he was jaundiced; I did his LFTs and they were off the scale. He lied to me at first and said he was only a social drinker, but finally he admitted that he uses vodka to cope with stress at work and has been drinking way too much for several years.' He sighed. 'I'm hoping it's going to turn out to be hepatitis rather than cirrhosis, but he's going to need a lot of help to give up the alcohol. He'll probably need medication to support him as well as counselling.'

Which was one of the things Abigail worried about with her father. Keith Brydon drank too much and had done so for years; it went with the rock-and-roll lifestyle. And she worried constantly that she'd be called by another hospital's emergency department because he'd collapsed. Hepatitis, a heart attack, a stroke—she worried about all of them. 'Poor guy. I assume you admitted him to the main wards?'

'Yes. They're going to give him steroids to reduce the inflammation of the liver. The poor guy's got a hard road ahead of him.' Lewis looked bleak. 'Some people are too proud to ask for help when they're stressed and struggling. And they're the ones who end up in our department—if they're lucky.'

'And we can do something to help,' she said. 'You spent time talking to him tonight, didn't you?'

He nodded. 'Sorry.'

'Don't be. I would've done the same.' Especially because the situation echoed her own worst fears.

'Thanks for being understanding.' He shook himself. 'And I'll stop being maudlin.'

When their meals arrived, he looked at her plate. 'That looks gorgeous.' He sighed. 'I wish I'd ordered something vegetarian now. It isn't fair to ask you for a taste when I can't reciprocate.'

'Sure you can.'

But offering him a taste from her fork turned out to be a mistake. It felt oddly intimate. And then she managed to spill butter down his shirt because her hand was shaking. 'Sorry. I, um…I'm not usually this clumsy.'

He laughed. 'Things come in threes, so you need to spill your coffee next.'

She felt her face flame. 'Sorry.'

'Abby, I was teasing. It doesn't matter. Everyone spills things.'

Maybe, but she hated being less than perfect. 'I'll pick up the dry-cleaning bill.'

He shook his head. 'There's no need. It'll come out in the wash.'

She could offer to wash his shirt for him, but then she'd probably manage to shrink it or something. What was it about this man that made her such a klutz? She bit her lip.

'Abby. It's not a problem. Chill,' he said.

She gave him a rueful smile. 'I don't get out much. And I guess it shows.'

'Good music, good food, good company. I don't see anything wrong in that,' he said.

Was he really nice at heart, or was he a shallow player? She wasn't sure, so she just smiled back at him.

'So what made you want to be a doctor?' he asked.

'Sydney and Marina were telling me this theory over lunch that we're doctors because we like fixing things,' she said.

'They're probably right.' He raised an eyebrow. 'You had lunch with them?'

She nodded. 'I would've gone to the bowling thing tonight with them, if I hadn't had these tickets.'

He smiled. 'Good. I'm glad you're getting to know the team better. They're a nice bunch.' He paused. 'What I don't get is why you're in the emergency department. I would've put you in family medicine.'

She raised an eyebrow. 'You don't think I'm tough enough to cope with emergency medicine?'

'No, it's not that. You're good at your job. But the way you were with that guy with anthrax the other day made me think you'd be good at cradle-to-grave medicine. You built a relationship with your patient. We don't get to do that in the emergency department—we rarely even know what happens to them once they leave us.'

Though, Lewis had spent time tonight settling a patient into the ward, and she'd just bet that he'd visit his patient over the weekend when he was on a break. 'I suppose not.'

He looked straight at her. 'So my guess is you chose emergency medicine because of your father.'

For a second Abigail forgot to breathe. Lewis had

looked her up on the Internet and made the connections. He must've done. Why else would he say something like that? 'What makes you say that?' she asked carefully.

'Because playing a round of golf a couple of times a week isn't going to make up for the rest of the lifestyle.'

She went cold. So Lewis *did* know who she was. And that was why he was here with her now. Not because he'd wanted to get to know her better or because he'd wanted to help her settle into the team. He was here because, just like all the other people she'd been stupid enough to go out with or even make friends with, he was more interested in her father. 'Lifestyle?' she asked slowly.

'Sitting in an office chair all day and either grabbing the wrong kind of sandwich or going out for lunch with a client or colleagues and having all three courses. With butter spread way too thickly on the bread and a generous helping of cream on the pudding.'

She blinked at him. What was he talking about? Wasn't it obvious that her father's lifestyle meant not taking enough exercise, eating too much of the wrong kind of food at weird times and a body-clock-breaking routine? Not to mention the other stuff that came with a rock-and-roll lifestyle. Alcohol. Tobacco. Recreational drugs—well, not that her father did those nowadays. She shook her head to clear it. 'What?'

'Businessmen of your father's generation. Given that you live in a very nice part of Pimlico, I'm guessing you're from the stockbroker belt.'

Oh. So he *didn't* know who her father was. He thought her father was a stockbroker. She nearly laughed. Her father commissioned a stockbroker, but no way did Keith Brydon live the stockbroker life himself. Her worries were different ones: even though her father didn't do drugs, there were still huge risks associated with his lifestyle.

'And your family home's a mansion in the home counties,' he said.

That part was true. Her father did have a mansion in the home counties. And a swimming pool that people had driven a car into before now, in true rock-star cliché style. 'Something like that,' she said. And she needed to get the topic off herself. Fast. 'What about you? Why did you pick emergency medicine?'

'You pinned me down on that earlier. I'm an adrenalin fiend,' he said.

She shook her head. 'I don't buy that. You're good with kids—you're patient and you listen. And, given that you refer to your sisters as your girls...'

Ice trickled down Lewis's spine. He'd seen Abigail at work so he knew she thought outside the box. She was bright enough to work it out for herself. Especially because he'd shot his mouth off earlier, talking about stress and people being too proud to ask for the help they needed.

'That's because they're my little sisters,' he said lightly.

'Mmm. But you talk about them more as if...' She paused, looking thoughtful.

All he had to do now was change the topic of conversation. Talk about music. Something. *Anything.*

But the words spilled out of his mouth. 'As if what?'

'As if you were involved in bringing them up.'

His chest felt tight. Hell. This was his own fault. He'd known that Abby could be dangerous to his peace of mind. Why hadn't he just left it? Why hadn't he made up something plausible? 'My dad died when we were young,' he said. 'I was the oldest, so I helped my mum.'

Except it hadn't really been help, had it? He'd made things so much worse in the long run.

She reached across the table and squeezed his hand briefly. 'That's rough on you.'

'I didn't mind helping out.'

'No, I mean losing your dad young. That's hard. You were close to him?'

He nodded. 'My dad was the best.' Please don't let her ask about his mother. Please don't let her guess that Fay Gallagher had gone completely to pieces and her fourteen-year-old son had been the one to keep the family together.

'And I'd guess it was an accident?'

Say yes. Tell her yes. Don't let her any closer. An all-out lie would be just fine here and now.

But it was as if his mouth wasn't listening to his head. The way she'd squeezed his hand like that—it was empathy, not pity. As if she knew what it was like. 'He had leukaemia.' He looked away. 'Three weeks after he was diagnosed, he was dead.' It had been so sudden. So shockingly sudden. None of them had been able to take it in. To cope.

Except him. Because he'd had to.

'I'm sorry. For bringing back bad memories.'

He waved a dismissive hand. 'I was the one who started the conversation.'

'And you're right about the lifestyle thing.' She sighed. 'I do worry about my dad. He never listens to a word I say, and I know he's never going to give up the cigars or the brandy, but I do try talking him into eating healthily and taking some sensible exercise to help take care of his heart.'

'Is that why you're vegetarian? You're trying to set him a good example?'

She laughed. 'Dad's not one to follow anyone else's example. He says salad is rabbit food. And the only way he'll eat spinach is if it's cooked in butter with a ton of parmesan on top, which pretty much loses the point of having spinach in the first place.' She shook her head. 'When I was in my teens, I had a friend whose family owned a farm. I stayed with them, and—well, when you've fed a calf with a bottle, you just can't...' She glanced at the lasagne on his plate. 'Um. I think I'll shut up now.'

'I think,' he said softly, 'we need to change the topic of conversation. Something much, much lighter, for both of us.'

'Good idea,' she said feelingly.

They spent the rest of the evening talking about music. Although Lewis was aware of a slight reticence on Abigail's part, he put it down to a bit of residual shyness. After all, music was hardly a contentious subject, was it?

He insisted on seeing her home to her flat in Pimlico.

She paused outside the door. 'Would you like to come in for coffee?'

Tempting. So very, very tempting.

But their conversation that evening had rattled him. He needed time to get his head together. He couldn't risk spilling any more of his guts to her. Particularly as Abigail Smith was starting to stir up feelings in him he'd buried for years and years.

'Thanks, but I need to get back.'

'OK.' She smiled at him, but it was the most fake smile he'd ever seen. Clearly she thought he was making an excuse because he didn't want to be with her.

In a way, it was true. Right now he didn't want to be with her. But it wasn't because he didn't like her—it was because he didn't trust himself. But how could he explain that without going into detail he really didn't want to share?

'Thanks for this evening. I really did enjoy it.' He brushed her cheek with the backs of his fingers. 'Even when you spilled stuff all over me.'

She blushed spectacularly, looking so adorable that Lewis temporarily lost his common sense. He leaned over and brushed his mouth against hers. The lightest, sweetest kiss he'd ever given anyone.

And then she was staring at him, all wide-eyed.

Oh, hell. He was making a real mess of this.

'I probably shouldn't have done that, Abby. I apologise.'

'Uh-huh.'

He couldn't read her expression. Was she annoyed because she thought he was trying to take advantage of her? Or did she think that he was pushing her away? Or...?

'I'm sorry,' he said again, and walked away. While he still could.

CHAPTER FIVE

ABIGAIL TOLD HERSELF not to overthink it. She should pretend that nothing had happened. Except whenever she drifted off to sleep for the next week she kept replaying the moment that Lewis's mouth had moved against hers.

Worse still, it gave her X-rated dreams. And it was a real struggle to be professional at work and act as if that kiss hadn't happened. Even though she knew he spelled trouble, Lewis had put her on a slow burn and she had no idea how to stop it.

On the Thursday evening her mobile phone beeped to signal a text message.

Are you busy on Sunday? L.

To her relief, she didn't have to lie. She'd already arranged to go and see her father. *Sorry. Doing family stuff. A.*

She thought that would be the end of it, but then her mobile phone actually rang.

She looked at the display, frowned, and answered it. 'Lewis? Why are you calling me?'

'Your social skills need some work, Abby,' he retorted. 'You're supposed to say hello and how nice it is to hear from me.'

'Hello, Lewis. How nice it is to hear from you.'

He laughed. 'And you're meant to say it with a bit of conviction. But I guess it's a start.'

'Right. What do you want?'

'OK, so you're busy on Sunday. But I also know you're off duty on Monday.'

'And?'

'And I wondered if you fancied joining me in some adrenalin-fiend stuff.'

This was her cue to make an excuse. To be sensible and stay well clear of him outside work.

But she couldn't help wanting to know what he had in mind. 'You want to go zip-lining again?'

'Better than that.'

She sighed. 'That's not enough detail for me to be able to make an informed decision, Lewis.'

He laughed. 'Tough. It's all you're getting, princess.'

'So you want me to trust you that I'll enjoy whatever this is?' Then a nasty thought hit her. 'Three dates and you're out, right?' And this would be the third.

'Technically, we're not dating,' he pointed out.

'You paid for a date with me. And then we went to the concert. This makes number three.'

'A paid-for date doesn't count. And that concert was just because you had a spare ticket.'

And he'd kissed her.

OK, so it hadn't been a full-blown smooch. But there had been something sweet and intimate about it. It hadn't been the kind of kiss you gave a colleague— or even a friend. It had been an exploratory kiss. Promising. Tempting.

Plus there was the way he'd held her hand during the concert…

'Is *this* a date?' she asked gingerly.

'No. It's part of my project to get you doing more team stuff.'

She scowled. 'I *am* doing more team stuff, I'll have you know. I have lunch with Sydney and Marina every Wednesday, and I'm going ice skating with the team next week. Plus it's really insulting to be considered somebody's project.'

He laughed. 'OK. I take that bit back. Come and do something exciting with me, Abby.'

She thought of that kiss and shivered. Right at that moment she couldn't speak.

'Abby?'

'I'm still here.'

'Come and play with me.' His voice was like melted chocolate. Sinful and tempting. Irresistible.

No. *Say no.*

But she really, really wanted to go with him. Would it be so bad just to have some uncomplicated fun, for a change? 'OK.'

'Great. I'll pick you up at half past nine.'

'Why can't I pick you up?'

'Because I'm more used to the adrenalin rush than you are, so I'll need to drive us home.' He paused. 'Unless you want to insure your car for me so I can drive you home afterwards. That'd work.'

She blew out a breath. 'I'm beginning to think I might've been a bit rash, agreeing to do whatever this is.'

'No, you haven't. I promise you'll enjoy it.'

'What if I don't?'

'Then I'll buy you an ice cream.'

She couldn't help laughing. 'Lewis, I'm thirty years old, not three.'

'You're never too old for ice cream, Abby. One last thing. Do you have asthma?'

'No. Why?'

'Just asking. See you at work tomorrow.'

'See you.'

She was still smiling when she cut the connection. Though she had a nasty feeling that she'd just agreed to a date with Lewis, even if they weren't calling it that.

Well, everyone in her life had always said she was too serious. Maybe Lewis would be good for her. He could teach her to lighten up a bit.

Her smile faded. No wonder he thought of her as his project. So, no, it wasn't a date. He had other motivations for going out with her on Monday. And part of them involved indulging himself in adrenalin-fiend stuff. She'd better remember that.

Lewis texted Abigail on the Sunday evening to tell her to wear a T-shirt, leggings and trainers—not jeans or boots. She knew there was no point in asking him why because he wouldn't tell her. And he wouldn't even tell her where they were going on Monday morning until he turned into a side road and she saw the sign for the airfield.

'Why are we going to an airfield?' She groaned. 'Please don't tell me you're one of those people who likes looking at planes.'

'As a matter of fact, I do. And steam engines.'

Was he teasing her? She couldn't be sure. He had a perfectly straight face. And he was wearing sunglasses so she couldn't see his eyes. She couldn't read him at all. 'You said we were doing something exciting.'

He grinned. 'We're not looking at planes, Abby. We're going up in one.'

'Oh.' So this was going to be a nice pleasure flight in a small plane. Well, that worked for her. She'd flown in small planes before now, in parts of the world he'd probably never even been to. Not that she could tell him that without explaining about her father, and she wasn't ready to do that. She didn't want things to change between them.

He parked the car and shepherded her to the office. 'Lewis Gallagher and Abigail Smith. We have a booking for a tandem skydive.'

Abigail was too shocked to take it in at first. But when he'd finished signing the forms and directed her to do the same, she narrowed her eyes at him. 'You said we were going up in a plane.'

'We are.'

'You didn't say we were jumping out of one!'

'Relax, Abby.' He patted her arm. 'It's a tandem skydive. You'll be strapped to a qualified instructor, so it's perfectly safe. The instructor is the one who controls the parachute and landing so all you have to do is enjoy the experience.'

It mollified her slightly. 'OK. So do we go and meet the instructor now?'

'Um, actually, you've already met him.'

She stared at him, frowning. 'When?'

He spread his hand, gave her a real mischievous little-boy grin and pointed to himself.

'What? But…you said I'd be with a qualified instructor.'

'You will be. I'm qualified.'

She couldn't take this in. 'But how? You're a doctor.'

* * *

Fair point. He knew he needed to reassure her. 'I had a gap year.' Six of them, actually, but she didn't need to know that much detail. 'I worked at a training centre—one of those outdoor places. We used to run management courses, the sort where the delegates have to do things outside their comfort zone and bond as a team. One of the activities we did was tandem skydiving. So I qualified as an instructor.'

She rolled her eyes. 'Trust an adrenalin fiend to find that kind of job for a gap year.'

Part of Lewis wanted her to keep thinking he was shallow. But part of him wanted her to know who he really was—and that was odd. He never usually wanted to let anyone get that close. He really ought to stay away from her but something about her drew him.

'Come on. We need to go to the briefing. What you need to know is that you'll be harnessed to my front. We'll jump at fifteen thousand feet and freefall for a minute, then I'll open the canopy and we'll land about five minutes later.'

Her eyes went wide. 'What if the parachute doesn't open?'

It was the question everybody asked. 'There's a reserve parachute. And there's an automatic activation device that opens it at lower altitudes if I haven't already deployed it.'

She blew out a breath. 'Do I need a mask or anything?'

'No. We're only going up to fifteen thousand feet, so there's plenty of oxygen. And even though we'll be falling at about a hundred and twenty miles an hour, the air doesn't actually enter your lungs at that speed. Though you'll have a helmet and goggles.'

'Right. And that's why you asked me about asthma.'

'Yep.' He touched her cheek with the backs of his fingers to reassure her. 'It's an amazing feeling. But it's not like going over the edge of a roller coaster. It's like floating in a swimming pool, except you can see for miles and miles and miles.'

'And you're qualified,' she checked.

'Yes. I do regular training sessions to keep my qualifications up to date. But if you'd rather go with someone else, I understand and I won't have a tantrum about it.'

She shook her head. 'Why didn't you offer something like this at the hospital auction?'

'Would you have bid for it?' he asked.

'Well—no,' she admitted.

'There's your answer, then. Ready to go?'

'I guess.'

'Good.' He squeezed her hand. 'You're going to enjoy this. I promise.'

Abigail wasn't so sure. Jumping out of a plane. It was so far outside the kind of thing she normally did.

And Lewis had surprised her. She'd had no idea that he was a qualified skydiver. Did anyone else at the hospital know? She had a feeling they probably didn't. There was a lot, lot more to Lewis than she'd thought. And she didn't understand why he kept it so quiet. Surely this would fit in with his reckless, dare-devil, party-boy image?

The briefing went through all the health and safety aspects of the flight, explaining exactly what was going to happen and what she needed to do to help the instructor. Then she was kitted out with a bright orange jumpsuit, helmet, goggles and gloves—as was Lewis.

'If only your harem at the hospital could see you now,' she teased. 'Very sexy, Dr Gallagher.'

He gave her a pained look. 'First of all, I don't have a harem. Secondly, this isn't about looking good, it's about safety.' And then he knocked her completely off balance by leaning forward and kissing the tip of her nose. 'Though you happen to look really cute.'

Cute?

The only person who ever said she was cute was her father—and that was because fathers were meant to say that sort of thing. Certainly none of her previous partners had called her cute.

Except Lewis wasn't actually her partner.

And how could she look cute in something that clashed so badly with her hair?

She was only half listening when he helped her on with the harness.

'Pay attention, Dr Smith,' he said. 'What did I just say?'

'I don't have a clue,' she admitted. And she really hoped that he put it down to nerves about doing one of his adrenalin-fiend things rather than the fact that he'd put her into a flat spin by kissing the end of her nose like that.

'I said we'll attach your harness to mine when we get to the plane. Now we're going to walk to the plane. Are you OK about this?'

'I think so.' She shivered.

'Scared?'

She nodded.

He grinned. 'It's awesome. I guarantee you'll be bubbling over when we're on the ground again.'

Well, he'd been right about the zip-lining. Maybe he'd be right about this, too.

Once in the plane, they attached her harness to his. Lewis wrapped his arms round her waist and rested his chin on her shoulder, and Abigail wasn't sure what made her pulse race more: the way he was holding her or the fact that they were going to be throwing themselves out of the plane very shortly.

As they got to the landing site, the doors opened. There was a rail above the door, and Lewis held on to it. The only thing stopping Abigail falling out of the doorway and plummeting down fifteen thousand feet was the harness that held them together. A little piece of webbing.

She was going to have to trust Lewis now like she'd never trusted anyone in her life before. And that scared her more than anything else.

'Ready?' he asked.

Not in a million years. 'Yes,' she muttered.

'Let's go,' he said, and they were out in the open air. Face down and falling.

Abigail remembered what they'd said at the briefing: she bent her lower legs back and stretched her arms out.

Adrenalin sizzled through her as they fell. Lewis was right; this wasn't like zip-lining or a roller coaster. It was just the two of them, with the earth spread out below them and a view like she'd never seen before—a total panorama with little fluffy white clouds scudding below them. She could see for miles and miles and miles, and it was breathtaking.

She loved every second of the freefall. But just as she

was starting to worry about how far and how fast they were falling, she felt Lewis pull the cord and heard the parachute open. It jerked them back up in the air, and the rest of the descent was much slower. Peaceful. Like nothing she could ever have imagined.

As they neared the ground, she lifted her legs up as they'd been instructed to do, and the next thing she knew they'd landed. Not skidding along the field, as she'd half expected, but gracefully.

Once Lewis was sure that she was steady on her feet, he detached his harness from hers and she was free to move. She turned to face him.

'So did you enjoy it?' he asked.

Her smile felt as if it was a mile wide. 'I *loved* it.' Adrenalin was pumping through her veins, and she couldn't help wrapping her arms round him and lifting her face up to his.

The next thing she knew, he was kissing her. Really kissing her. Not like that tentative, skin-tingling brush against her mouth from last time: this was a full-on, no-holds-barred kiss.

Her toes curled and she felt as if her knees had melted. But he was holding her, making sure she wouldn't fall. Or was he holding on to her for dear life? She didn't have a clue. She couldn't think straight. All she could do was feel.

And Lewis Gallagher kissed like a fallen angel.

When he finally broke the kiss, they just stared at each other. There was a slash of colour over his cheekbones, his eyes were wide, the pupils huge, and his mouth was reddened. Abigail was pretty sure she looked the same.

What now?

It felt as if they'd been frozen for ever. But then he coughed. 'I'd better sort out the parachute.'

'Can I help?'

'Thanks, but it's quicker for me to do it than to talk you through it,' he said.

Feeling a bit like a spare part, she watched him pack up the parachute then walked back to the office with him to sort out the last bit of admin.

He didn't say a word until they were both sitting in his car.

And then he turned to her, looking serious. 'Abby, what happened just now on the field—'

'Shouldn't have happened,' she cut in swiftly. Before he could say it. And no way could she look him in the eye. She didn't want him to know how much that kiss had affected her.

Abigail looked drawn. Ashen.

Oh, hell. He really shouldn't have kissed her like that. He'd been way out of line.

Then again, she'd kissed him back. And Lewis had a feeling that she was just as mixed up about it as he was. 'I know. But it did.' He paused. It was time to be honest. 'And I think it's going to happen again.'

That made her look at him. And she was all wide-eyed and beautiful. He wanted to kiss her again right at that moment, until they were both too dizzy to know where they were.

'We're colleagues,' she said.

He noticed she didn't put the word 'just' in there. Because she obviously knew they were more than that, too.

'Abby,' he said softly, 'I find you attractive. Really attractive. And I think it's mutual.'

She said nothing. He sighed inwardly. He had a

pretty good idea what was bugging her: his reputation. Three dates and you're out. She'd even said it when he'd phoned her to talk her into spending today with him.

The grapevine had it wrong. He didn't date anywhere near as many women as everyone seemed to believe, and he didn't break things off that quickly, either. And he didn't promise any more than he could offer. He just wasn't looking for commitment.

He ought to be sensible about this. Back off.

But Abigail drew him. Beneath that quiet, shy exterior was a woman with as much zest for life as he had. And he wanted to know why she kept it under wraps.

'Abby, I can take you home right now,' he said. 'But I think you're going to spend the rest of the day feeling the same way that I will.'

She looked at him again. 'Which is?'

He couldn't put it into words. But he could show her. He leaned forward and kissed her stupid.

When they came up for air, she was shaking. 'Oh, my God. I haven't been kissed in a car like that since I was a teenager. If then.'

'Guess what? I haven't kissed anyone in a car like that since I was—well, not that much older than a teenager.' Not since the girl who had broken his heart. Not that he was going to think of Jenna now. That part of his life was over. She was irrelevant.

He rubbed his thumb along Abigail's lower lip. 'So, what now, Abby? Do you want me to take you home? Or can I tempt you back to mine for lunch? I was planning asparagus and home-made hollandaise sauce.'

He could tempt her, Abigail thought. With a lot of things. And this would be the most stupid thing she'd ever done.

She knew Lewis didn't do commitment, and he was the worst person she could possibly get involved with—an adrenalin fiend who wouldn't take things seriously.

'Asparagus,' she said slowly. 'With home-made hollandaise sauce.'

'Or butter and freshly shaved parmesan.' He leaned forward and stole another kiss. 'Anything you want.'

She could say no.

Or she could be brave. She could tell him what she wanted.

'Anything I want?' she checked.

He nodded. 'Tell me what you want, Abby.'

She lifted her hand to cup his cheek. 'You, Lewis. I want *you*.'

His eyes went all dark and stormy and he moved his face to press a kiss into her palm before folding her fingers around his kiss. 'If I get a speeding fine on the way home, woman, I hope you know it'll be all your fault,' he said.

She laughed, and her last doubts dissolved.

CHAPTER SIX

BUT ABIGAIL'S DOUBTS came back when they became stuck in traffic, and she was silent all the way back from the traffic jam to Lewis's flat.

'This was all meant to be spontaneous,' he grumbled. 'Sorry. I should've taken a different route home.'

'It's OK.'

'You don't sound OK.' He sighed. 'Spit it out, Abby.'

'Three dates and you're out. I was just thinking—is there any point in even *starting* this?'

He rolled his eyes. 'The grapevine gets everything out of proportion. For your information, I've dated some women more than three times.'

'And some less than that, so it evens out.'

'I guess so,' he admitted. 'But I don't actually date that many women, whatever the grapevine says. And I definitely don't sleep with every woman I date.' He paused. 'Not everyone wants to settle down and get married and have a family. Just so you know, I don't.'

She thought about it. Was that what she wanted? What she'd never quite had, growing up?

And what had made Lewis wary of relationships, given that he was clearly close to his sisters and was a doting uncle? Why didn't he want a family? If she asked, she had a feeling that he'd change the subject. They really didn't know each other well enough for this kind of conversation. And it wasn't appropriate anyway—strictly speaking, they weren't even dating.

She needed to know where she stood. 'So this is a fling?' she asked.

He raked a hand through his hair. 'I don't know. I don't know what the hell it is.'

'You said I was your project.' That still stung.

He kissed her; she thought it was probably just to shut her up. Then he sighed. 'Yes. No. I have no idea.' He stared at her, his eyes stormy. 'What is it about you that puts me in a flat spin? I'm not used to this.'

That little admission of vulnerability, added to the way he looked so appealingly rumpled, widened the crack round her heart. She leaned over to kiss him.

When he broke the kiss, he said, 'Abby, you have a choice. I can take you home.'

'Or?'

'I can take you to bed.' His voice was low and gravelly and incredibly sexy.

She had a pretty good idea what he wanted her to say but she liked the fact that he was giving her the choice, rather than expecting her just to fall in with his wishes. She smiled. 'I'm really glad we had the roof up on the way back.'

He frowned. 'Why?'

'Because it'll take us less time to get from your car to your flat.'

In answer, he kissed her, putting her into the same flat spin he'd claimed she'd put him in. She barely registered that they'd left the car until he fumbled with the keys on the doorstep, dropped them and swore. 'Sorry.'

She stroked his cheek. 'I work in the emergency department. I've heard much worse than that.'

'I know. But even so, I shouldn't swear in front of you.'

Clearly he'd been brought up the old-fashioned way. With family values. So why was he turning his back on them when it came to his personal life?

'I'm sorry,' he said again.

The second he closed the door behind them he kissed her again. Her back was against the wall, his arms were wrapped round her and his mouth was moving against hers. Tiny, nibbling, teasing kisses along her lower lip, tempting and demanding and offering, all at the same time.

She opened her mouth to let him deepen the kiss, and everything around her seemed to fade. All she was aware of was Lewis and the way he was kissing her.

He broke the kiss. 'I can't wait any more, Abby. I'm burning up for you.'

To her shock, he actually scooped her up and carried her to his bedroom. Literally sweeping her off her feet. Nobody had ever done that to her before.

She was still registering that when he set her down on her feet again, making sure that her body was in full contact with his all the way and she was left in no doubt about his arousal.

'You're beautiful,' he said. Gently, he removed the elastic she used to tie her hair back. 'And your hair is amazing.' He ran his fingers through her hair. 'So soft and smooth and silky.'

'Dead straight and ginger.' It had earned her a fair bit of teasing when she'd finally gone to school. But her attempt at going blonde and curly had been a disaster.

She'd ended up having her hair cut horrendously short and it had taken her two years to grow it back. Since then she'd kept it tied back and had had done nothing more than have the ends trimmed.

'Copper,' he corrected. 'And my sisters would kill to have hair that's naturally straight like this and doesn't need to be tamed with a pair of straighteners.'

He liked her hair?

The surprise must have shown in her face because he rubbed his thumb along her lower lip. 'You're beautiful. But I need to see more of you, Abby. I need you naked and in my bed, with that glorious hair spread over my pillow. Right now.'

The sheer desire in his eyes sent a thrill through her. He meant it. And he saw her for herself.

She nodded and lifted her arms up. He slid his fingers underneath the hem of her T-shirt and slowly drew the material over her head.

'Gorgeous,' he said, his voice hoarse, and traced the lacy edge of her bra, his fingertips skimming over her skin and making her feel super-heated.

'My turn.' She stripped off his T-shirt in the same way. 'Very nice,' she said, splaying her hands against his bare chest. He had perfect musculature, with a light sprinkling of hair on his chest. She let her hands slide down his abdomen. 'That's a perfect six-pack, Dr Gallagher. You take care of yourself.'

'I try.' He smiled, then dipped his head and brushed his mouth against hers. 'My turn again?'

'I—um...' She looked awkwardly at him. 'My trainers are in the way.'

'I can do something about that.' He gave her a slow,

sexy smile. 'Though I have to admit I'd love to see you in high heels.'

She didn't have any. Abigail Smith wore sensible shoes and sensible clothes. She wasn't a vamp. So what on earth was she doing here, with the most eligible man in the hospital?

'Abby. Stop thinking.' He kissed her briefly. 'Right now you're everything I want. Fripperies don't matter.'

He dropped to his knees in front of her and dealt with the laces of her trainers, then peeled her leggings down. He took it maddeningly slowly, stroking her buttocks and thighs as he uncovered her skin, making her shiver.

She dragged in a breath. 'Socks. So not sexy.'

'I don't care. I've got a very nice view from here.' He looked up at her with heat in his eyes. 'But as the lady wishes.' He lifted one foot so he could remove her sock, caressing her instep as he bared it, then did the same with the other foot.

Since when had *feet* been sexy? Abigail had had no idea that feet could be an erogenous zone. But Lewis— Lewis made her feel like a siren.

'You look like one,' he said.

'What?'

'A siren. Especially with that amazing hair. I can see you as a mermaid, sitting on a rock and combing your hair in the sunshine.'

She groaned. 'Oh, no. I didn't mean to say that aloud.'

He pressed a kiss to the side of her knee, making her legs feel even weaker. 'It's cute. You're no ice princess, Abby. The grapevine's got you totally wrong. You're all woman. Sexy as hell. And I really, really want you.'

'I want you, too,' she said shakily. 'And you're wearing way more than I am.'

He got to his feet in one lithe movement. 'Do something about it, then.'

Her hands were trembling as she slid his tracksuit bottoms over his hips. The material pooled at his feet; she knelt down to unlace his trainers and finish removing his tracksuit bottoms. Then she rocked back on her haunches and looked at him. He was glorious. Like a Michelangelo sculpture.

'I need to kiss you, Abby,' he said. He took her hands and drew her to her feet, then cupped her face and caught her lower lip between his. She couldn't help responding, letting him deepen the kiss and matching him nibble for nibble, desire for desire.

She tangled her fingers in his hair; he slid his hands down over her shoulders, pushing the straps of her bra down. He deftly undid the clasp of her bra and let her breasts spill into his hands.

'You're seriously lush,' he said. 'And I can't wait any longer.' He picked her up and carried her over to the bed, nudging the duvet aside before he laid her on the mattress.

Then she realised that his curtains were open, and froze.

'Abby?'

She swallowed hard. 'Your curtains are open.'

He smiled and stole a kiss. 'Don't worry. Nobody can see in. My neighbours opposite are out at work. And it'd be a shame to shut the sunshine out.'

How could she resist the appeal in his beautiful slate-blue eyes?

She let him kiss her worries away. He kissed his way along her collar bones then down her sternum.

She arched towards him, and he smiled. 'What do you want me to do, Abby?'

'I…' She felt the colour staining her face.

'I can't read your mind,' he said softly. 'I know what I'd like to do. But it's what you'd like me to do that I'm more interested in.' He stole a kiss. 'If it pleases you, it pleases me as well.'

She swallowed hard. 'Touch me, Lewis.'

'Where?' His eyes darkened. 'Tell me, Abby.'

Her hand was shaking as she took his hand and placed it on her breast.

'Good choice,' he whispered, teasing her nipple with his thumb and forefinger. Then he dipped his head, took her nipple into his mouth and sucked.

Abigail sighed with pleasure and slid her fingers into his hair, urging him on.

She tipped her head back when he switched sides. 'More,' she whispered.

He slid one finger under the edge of her knickers and drew a fingertip along the length of her sex. When he touched her clitoris, she shivered.

'Like this?' he murmured against her ear.

It was as if he could read her mind and knew exactly how and where she liked being touched. And the way he was stroking her, teasing her, was making it impossible for her to speak a proper sentence. 'Uh.'

'Good.'

She was incoherent by the time he stopped; all she could do was open her eyes and look at him in mute appeal.

'Condom,' he said, vaulted off the bed and stripped off his underpants.

Abigail just stared at him. Naked, he was beautiful.

And right now he was all hers.

He rummaged in the pocket of his tracksuit bottoms for his wallet and extracted a small foil packet.

'Just so you know,' he said softly, 'there really aren't many notches on my bedpost. This isn't something I do every day or even every week.'

'I can't even remember the last time I did this.'

'"All work and no play",' he quoted with a smile. 'So I think we need to do each other a favour right now. I'd hate people to think of me as dull.'

She sat up, drawing her knees up and resting her chin on them. 'They don't.' And there was the rub. 'Whereas they know I am.'

'Dull?' He shook his head. 'No. You're not. Dull women don't go zip-lining. Or throw themselves out of planes. Or kiss me in a way that scrambles my brain. And you most definitely do.'

'Only because you talked me into it.'

'Abby.' He came to sit next to her, took her hand and pressed a kiss into the palm. Then he folded her fingers around it. 'You don't have to do this. I can take you home. Well, after I've cooked you lunch.'

And now it was all going horribly wrong. She wrapped her hands round her legs, curling into a near-fetal position. 'I think you were right about me,' she said miserably. 'I need to be someone's project.'

'No. You just need to have a little faith in yourself. You know you're a good doctor, right?'

'Yes.' She wasn't worried about her professional life. She worked hard, she knew what she was doing and she knew when to ask for help.

'And you're an interesting person.'

No. She was the daughter of someone interesting.

Even though she thought Lewis might understand that, she still didn't want to tell him who she really was. She made a noncommittal noise and looked away. 'Perhaps I'd better go.'

'Not yet.' To her surprise, he hauled her onto his lap. 'Right now, I think you need a cuddle.'

Since when had playboys been sensitive? 'Don't be nice to me. I might cry.'

'Shh.' He wrapped his arms round her and rested his cheek against hers.

She closed her eyes. He didn't say a word, just held her, and all her self-doubts began to melt away.

He dropped a kiss against her hair. 'Better?'

She nodded. 'Sorry. I'm being an idiot.'

'No, but I'd guess you've had a rubbish choice in men in the past,' he said dryly. 'As for the guy who made you feel you're dull—he didn't know you, Abby. Because you're *not* dull.' He took her hand and placed it against his chest so she could feel the rapid beat of his heart. 'A dull woman couldn't do that to me.'

But she could. She could make his blood heat.

'Kiss me, Lewis,' she said.

He pressed a soft, gentle kiss to the corner of her mouth.

'I mean properly.'

His eyes widened. 'You don't have to do this.'

'I want to,' she said. 'And this time I'm not going to back out. OK, so I had a bit of a wobble just now.'

'Hey. You jumped out of a plane this morning. You're allowed to have a wobble.'

God, that smile. It made her heart feel as if it had just done a backflip. Which was anatomically impossible. Lewis was impossible. This whole situation was ridiculous.

'Can we start again?' she asked.

'If you're sure you want to.'

'I am.'

This time he let her set the pace. He let her touch him, explore him, kiss her way around his body.

And when she was quivering, needing him inside her, she whispered, 'Now.'

In answer, he kissed her, ripped open the foil packet and rolled the condom onto his erect penis. Then he knelt between her thighs and eased his body into hers.

The first time it was meant to be embarrassing and awkward, second-guessing what each other liked.

But this—this felt *right*.

'OK?' he asked softly.

'Very OK.' She stroked his face. 'You're not bad at this.'

He laughed, and kissed her. 'I've hardly started.'

And then he proved it to her, by bringing her to a swift climax—then slowing down and making the tension build up and up and up, coiling inside her.

'Lewis, I can't…' This couldn't possibly happen again.

'Don't fight it, Abby. Open your eyes and look at me.'

She did, and her body tightened around his at the same time that she felt his body surge hard into hers.

This man took her breath away. He made her feel like nobody had ever made her feel before.

'Let me deal with the condom,' he said. 'And don't start thinking, Abby. I don't want a single doubt in your head when I get back here.' As if to make sure of it, he kissed her again, making her head spin.

She lay curled under the duvet, waiting for him. Lewis had been a real revelation. Sensitive, thoughtful, taking care of her needs. She really hadn't expected that.

How had he gotten a reputation as a heartbreaker? Or was that part of his defence mechanism? He'd said that he didn't want to get married and settle down. Acting like a heartbreaker was one way of making sure that his relationships didn't last that long.

'I said, don't start thinking,' he said softly, climbing back into bed beside her and drawing her into his arms.

'I'm not,' she fibbed.

'Never play poker,' he said. 'Your face is very expressive. You can't hide what you're thinking.'

Oh, yes, she could. And she'd learned how to play poker from one of the very best. Maybe, she thought, that was the way to get Lewis to tell her what was really in his head. Unpick the puzzle. She'd just bet he wouldn't be able to resist the challenge.

'Maybe,' she said, and turned her head to press a kiss into his shoulder. 'Thank you. You made me feel amazing.'

He stroked her face. 'That's because you are amazing.'

'I wasn't fishing for a compliment.'

'I know. Or I wouldn't have said it.'

She smiled at him. 'Thank you.'

He kissed her lightly. 'I promised you asparagus. Give me twelve minutes.'

'Do you want some help?'

'No. Stay there.'

'Here?' She blinked at him.

He gave her a look that made her temperature spike. 'I thought we could have lunch in bed.'

'Very decadent of you, Dr Gallagher.'

He just laughed, kissed her, and pulled on a pair of shorts. 'Butter and parmesan?'

'Yes, please.'

True to his word, he was back in twelve minutes with a tray containing a dish of dressed asparagus and a plate of good bread.

Not only was the food good, it was fun—because Lewis insisted on them feeding each other, and Abigail thoroughly enjoyed teasing him.

Though it was also messy. By the time they'd finished, they were both covered in melted butter.

'What a good excuse to have a shower with you,' Lewis said with a grin.

He proceeded to make love to her there, too. And Abigail didn't care that her hair went in rats' tails if it got wet and she didn't dry it properly. She was just enjoying being with Lewis. Pretending that the outside world didn't exist.

When they finally got dressed again, Lewis led her into his living room and pulled her onto his lap on the sofa.

'So where do we go from here?' she asked.

'I guess,' he said, 'we might be an item.'

'But?' She could hear it as clearly as if he'd said it out loud.

He sighed. 'The hospital grapevine might give us a bit of a hard time if this becomes common knowledge. I have this stupid reputation.'

She really wasn't sure whether he meant that he wanted to keep his reputation or whether he resented it. And if she asked him, she didn't think he'd tell her.

'So you want to keep it to ourselves?'

'Until we decide where this is taking us, that might be a good idea.' He kissed the tip of her nose. 'Which isn't a way of saying I'm ashamed of you. I'm not.'

'But you want to be my dirty little secret,' she said lightly.

'The ice princess dating the hospital Casanova. Yes.'

Was there a slight edge to his tone or was it her imagination? She stroked his face. 'Lewis. Why do you let people think you're something you're not?'

'It's easier that way.' He paused. 'So you don't think I'm like Casanova?'

'No, but I wouldn't mind seeing you dressed up as an eighteenth-century Venetian.' Then she looked at him. 'Tell me you didn't have a summer job as a gondolier, dressed as Casanova.'

'No. I missed a trick there, didn't I?' He smiled at her. 'I like you, Abby Smith.'

'I like you too, Lewis Gallagher.'

'Good.' He kissed her. 'So. Have you had enough of me for today or can I take you out to dinner?'

She glanced down at her T-shirt and leggings. 'You have a really bad habit of suggesting that when I'm really not dressed for dinner.'

'We can go back to your place and you can change. Or I can cook here.'

'You cooked lunch.' She paused. She was about to take a risk. But wasn't Lewis also taking a risk in starting a relationship with her? The man who didn't do commitment had said they were an item… 'Or we could have dinner at mine. I could cook for us.'

He looked pleased, and she realised that she'd been holding her breath, waiting for his reaction.

'That'd be good. Thank you.'

Back at her flat, she made him a coffee. To her relief, he went to the bathroom and that gave her time to remove the photograph on the mantelpiece—herself and her father in the back garden. She wasn't ready to tell Lewis about that. Not yet. Not until she felt much more secure about what was happening between them and her burgeoning friendships at work.

When he joined her in the living room, she said, 'Help yourself to the television and what have you.'

'Can I do anything to help?'

'No, it's fine.'

'Territorial about your kitchen?' he asked.

''Fraid so,' she admitted.

'Then I'm going to be nosy in your bookshelves.'

Abigail spent probably too much time in the kitchen, fussing, but eventually dinner was ready and she went through to the living room to call him in. 'Sorry—I've neglected you.'

He lowered the journal he was reading and smiled at her. 'No worries. It was nice to have the chance to catch up with some reading.'

She knew he took his work seriously, but it still surprised her that Lewis the party boy would opt for reading a serious medical journal over flicking through television channels. Then again, he'd surprised her a lot today.

'I know you're driving, but would you like a glass of wine?'

'I'll stick to a soft drink, if you don't mind.' He followed her through to the kitchen and sat at her small bistro table. 'That looks good.'

'Thank you. Though I have to admit to cheating and

using a sachet of pre-cooked quinoa to stuff the peppers.'

'It's lovely,' he said when he'd tasted it. 'I'll have to pinch the recipe for Dani.'

Being with him in her kitchen felt oddly intimate. And he was still pretty much a stranger. Her shyness flooded back; trying to combat it, she said, 'Shall I put some music on?'

'Sure. Given that you knew all the words to that song, the other week, I guess you're going to choose Brydon?'

All her Brydon CDs were signed copies. And if Lewis saw Keith's flamboyant signature and took a closer look, then read the inscription to Cinnamon, it would mean way too many explanations. Ones she wasn't quite ready to give. 'I'm in the mood for classical,' she said hastily.

'Fine by me.'

Funny. Even though he'd been to the concert with her and she knew he enjoyed classical, she'd been so sure he'd prefer dance music. She chose a Bach string quartet, then came back to the table.

'Very nice. I used to study to this,' Lewis said.

Abigail looked surprised. 'There's a lot more to you than meets the eye. Why do you let people think you're someone you're not?' she asked again.

He shrugged. 'It's easier.'

'You know what you were saying about my rubbish choice of men—I think that's true for you, too.'

Yeah. The woman he'd been so sure he could spend the rest of his life with. The one he'd met when his family commitments had been starting to ease and he'd been able to see his way clear to training as a doctor.

He'd proposed to Jenna. He'd even bought her a ring and asked her to wait for him to finish university. But she hadn't wanted to wait. She'd forced his hand—and she'd let him down in the worst possible way.

He shook himself. Not now. He forced himself to smile at Abigail and keep it light. 'Newsflash for you, princess. I don't date men.'

She rolled her eyes. 'You know what I mean.'

'We all make mistakes. I learned from mine.' And he didn't want to go into that now. He switched the conversation back to food, and to his relief she went with it.

When they'd finished the peppers, she brought out a bowl of mixed berries—raspberries, blueberries, cherries and strawberries. And she served it with a seriously good raspberry sorbet.

'Sorry, this is a bit lazy. I should've made a proper summer pudding,' she said.

'You weren't planning to cook me dinner, so you didn't have enough time to make a summer pudding—and, anyway, this is a healthier version. Much better.'

She gave him a grateful smile.

She wouldn't let him wash up after dinner. 'It won't take me five minutes. Let's go and sit down in the living room with some coffee.'

And Lewis was quite happy to curl up on the sofa with her and watch some old comedy re-runs. Weird. Usually, when he dated someone, he kept the evening short and sweet, not wanting to let her too close. But he'd spent the whole day with Abigail and he still didn't want to bolt.

Which should in itself be a warning.

He wasn't going to repeat the mistake he'd made with Jenna.

But the situation was different now. His sisters were grown up and his career was on track. His mother... well, some things you couldn't fix.

He kissed Abigail lightly. 'I'd better go.'

'Uh-huh.'

'Abby.' He kissed her lingeringly. 'Today's been amazing.'

'Mmm. It's not every day someone throws you out of a plane.'

He laughed. 'No, I jumped and you happened to be attached to me.' He traced her lower lip with the tip of his forefinger. 'And afterwards. That wasn't supposed to happen.'

'But I'm glad it did.'

That whispered admission warmed him. 'So am I.' He kissed her again. 'I'll see you tomorrow.'

'At work. In professional mode.'

'Absolutely, Dr Smith.'

And he really had to go, before he broke all his personal rules and asked if he could stay.

CHAPTER SEVEN

THE NEXT DAY at work, Abigail's pulse quickened as she saw Lewis.

'Good morning, Dr Smith,' he said.

So he'd meant it about keeping their relationship away from the eyes of the hospital grapevine. He was treating her as he always did, just as part of the team. She knew they'd agreed to that but it still put a lump of disappointment into her throat that he wasn't going to acknowledge their relationship. Which was ridiculous, and she was cross with herself for being so wet and needy. Was it any wonder that men didn't usually like her for herself?

'Good morning, Dr Gallagher,' she said, keeping her voice as professional as possible.

It didn't help that they were rostered together in Resus.

Or maybe it did, because it meant they were too busy to do anything other than think about their patients. Especially when a four-year-old was brought in with suspected acute asthma.

The little girl was too breathless to talk and her pulse was fast. Her mother was panicking, her voice high with fright as she explained what had happened.

Lewis introduced them both to Mrs Jones, his voice calm and reassuring. 'I know it's scary seeing Kirsty like this, but try not to worry. We're going to make her feel better. We need to treat her to help her breathing and we'll try to talk you through what we're doing as we go, but we need to focus on Kirsty first so we might not get a chance to explain everything. Once we've started the treatment we'll have time to answer all your questions.'

'Kirsty, sweetheart, my name's Dr Abby,' Abigail said. 'I'm going to put a special mask on you to help you breathe more easily.' She gently put the mask on the little girl, talking her thorough it and reassuring her, and administered high flow oxygen.

'Has anything like this ever happened before?' Lewis asked.

'No. We were round at my friend's. Kirsty was playing with their new kitten but then she started wheezing and couldn't breathe. I thought she'd swallowed something. I didn't know what to do so my friend drove me here. It wasn't far so we thought it'd be quicker than calling an ambulance.'

'You did absolutely the right thing in bringing her in,' Lewis said, squeezing her hand.

'I think Kirsty's just had a bad asthma attack,' Abigail said gently. 'And that can be very scary to see. Does anyone in the family have asthma?'

Mrs Jones shook her head.

'How about hay fever or eczema?' Lewis asked.

'I had eczema when I was tiny,' Mrs Jones told them. 'I have to be a bit careful about the washing powder I use, doing laundry, or it makes me itch. I always use non-bio. But Kirsty never had eczema.' She shook her head. 'I don't understand why she has asthma.'

'Often if a parent has asthma, eczema or hay fever, the child will have one of the three as well. It just might not be the same allergic reaction as the parent has,' Abigail explained.

Mrs Jones looked stricken. 'So it's my fault she can't breathe?'

'It's nobody's fault. It just happens. Don't blame yourself,' Lewis said. 'The main thing is we'll get her breathing back to normal, and then you can have a chat with the paediatrician and we'll sort out some medication.'

'You mean like a puffer? One of the boys in her pre-school group has one.'

'Yes. She'll have one she takes every day to prevent attacks and one she takes if she has an attack to stop the wheezing and coughing,' Abigail said. She stroked the little girl's hand. Kirsty's breathing seemed to be easing slightly. 'Kirsty, I need to you to do something very important for me. I'd like you to blow as hard as you can into a special tube. Can you do that for me?'

The little girl nodded.

Abby removed the mask so the little girl could blow into the expiratory flow meter. Just as she'd suspected, it was less than half of what it should've been so the asthma attack was a severe one.

'Thank you, Kirsty. That's brilliant. I'm going to give you some special medicine now through the mask, and all you have to do is breathe and it works,' she said.

'The medicine's going to help open her airways and make it easier for her to breathe,' Lewis told Mrs Jones.

Abigail fitted a nebuliser to the mask and added

salbutamol. 'You're being very brave, Kirsty. Can you swallow some medicine for me before I put the mask back on you?'

'Yeth,' the little girl lisped.

Quickly, Abigail gave her some oral prednisolone, then took out one of the stickers she kept in her pocket.'

Kirsty brightened at the sight of it. 'It's a star.'

'Which I only give to really brave little girls. I think you deserve this.' She gave the sticker to the little girl, who immediately took off the backing and stuck it to her T-shirt.

'And now I need to put a special machine on your finger now. It's a bit like a glove. It won't hurt, but it helps me see if the medicine is working or if I need to give you a different one. Is that all right?'

Kirsty nodded.

'It's a light beam through that goes through a sensor to measure the oxygen in her blood,' Lewis said to Mrs Jones. 'It won't hurt.'

'So is she going to be all right?' Mrs Jones asked.

'Yes. She has asthma. What happens is that when Kirsty comes into contact with something that triggers the asthma, the muscles round the wall of her airways tighten up. That makes the airways narrower and that's why it's hard for her to breathe,' Lewis said.

'What caused it?' Mrs Jones asked.

'I'd say the most likely thing that triggered today's attack would be your friend's kitten,' Abigail said.

Mrs Jones frowned. 'But she's played with the cat before and never had problems.'

'That often happens. Sometimes it takes years from the first time you come in contact with something you're allergic to until you actually have an asthma at-

tack,' Lewis explained. 'You might find she's sensitive
to other furry animals or birds. The paediatrician will
discuss this with you and set up a personal action plan
to help you keep an eye on Kirsty's asthma, so you'll
know what to do if you think her symptoms are getting worse.'

After a quarter of an hour Kirsty seemed to be im-
proving. 'We're going to keep her on oxygen and the
medicine in the nebuliser until the paediatrician's seen
her,' Abigail said. 'But the good news is that she's responding well and I'm pretty sure you'll be able to talk
to her tonight.'

The triage nurse came into the cubicle. 'Sorry to in-
terrupt. Just to let you know that Dr Morgan's here when
you're ready to see her,' she said quietly.

'Thanks. We're ready now,' Abigail said.

When the paediatrician came in, Abigail introduced
Katrina Morgan to Mrs Jones and Kirsty.

'We'll leave you with Dr Morgan now,' she said.
'She'll take you up to the ward where they can keep an
eye on Kirsty for a little bit longer, and she'll be able to
help you with the treatment plan.' She smiled at Kirsty.
'You take care now.'

'Bye, Dr Abby.' The little girl waved shyly.

'You were very good with Kirsty's mum,' Abigail
said to Lewis when they were out of earshot. 'You really calmed her down.'

'You know as well as I do that children respond better to treatment if their parents aren't panicking.' He
smiled. 'And you were very good with Kirsty. I noticed
you called yourself Dr Abby to her.'

'Let's just say your project's working,' she said dryly.

'Good.' He laughed. 'So you have a secret supply of shiny stickers, do you?'

'It's just from one of the stationery chains, not a special order or anything.'

He sighed. 'It's a girl thing, isn't it? My sisters can't pass stationery shops either. I bet you have one of those pens with the feathery bit on the end.'

She laughed. 'I do indeed. As you say, it's a girl thing.'

'Do you—?' he began, then shook his head. 'We'd better get on.'

What had he been about to ask her?

But she didn't get the chance to push him further, and he didn't suggest having lunch together or seeing her after work.

Maybe he'd changed his mind and he wanted to go back to being just colleagues. Well, she'd just have to deal with it. It wasn't as if she hadn't been warned that Lewis Gallagher didn't do commitment.

Lewis didn't call or text her that evening either, and Abigail didn't call him as she didn't want him to think she was clingy or pushy. He was in Resus the next day while she was on Minors so she didn't get the chance to see him at work either.

'You're quiet, Abby. Is everything OK?' Marina asked her at lunch on Wednesday.

'Yes, I'm fine,' Abigail fibbed. 'I'm looking forward to the team night out on Friday. I've never been ice skating.'

'I'm absolutely hopeless,' Sydney said. 'But my goal this time is to get round the edge of the whole rink, even if I have to hold on, and not fall over more than ten times.'

Marina laughed. 'I'm not much better, Syd. Max is surprisingly good, though.'

Abigail would just bet that Lewis was good, too. She wasn't sure whether he was going or not and didn't want to ask Marina or Sydney in case they wanted to know why she was so interested. She was happy to let the two other doctors chatter on and stayed in the background. But it was bugging her that Lewis had been practically ignoring her since they'd made love. She could see now why he drove women crazy.

He finally called her that evening. 'Hey, princess. Are you busy?'

She was tempted to say yes and put the phone down, but that would be childish. And she didn't want him to know how put out she was that he was keeping their relationship a secret at work. 'Don't call me "princess". It's annoying. And, yes, I'm busy.'

'What are you doing?'

'Watching a movie, if you must know.' And she hated the fact that she sounded so prim and snotty. That wasn't her. At all.

'If I bring a tub of posh ice cream, can I come and join you?'

'It's a rom-com. You'll hate it. Anyway, you've already missed the first half an hour, so there isn't much point in seeing the rest.'

'I don't mind.' She could almost hear the smile in his voice. 'If I'm honest, it's just an excuse to come and lie on your sofa with you in my arms.'

'You're taking a lot for granted.'

'You really have had a bad day, haven't you?'

'No.' She sighed. 'Lewis…'

'Let me come over. I'll bring ice cream. What do you like?'

She gave in. 'Anything except chocolate.'

'You don't like chocolate?' He sounded surprised.

'I like chocolate, and I like ice cream. But I don't like chocolate ice cream,' she corrected. 'I know it's weird.'

'It is. Seriously weird. Chocolate's my favourite. OK. I'll be with you in about twenty minutes. Don't hold the film for me.'

In exactly twenty minutes Lewis rang her doorbell. 'Hey, beautiful.' He kissed her hello and handed her a tub of posh strawberry ice cream.

'Thank you.'

He narrowed his eyes. 'Right. Spit it out.'

'Spit what out?'

'I take back what I said about you having a rough day at work. You're annoyed about something.'

'What makes you say that?'

'Your eyes have a really dark ring round them.'

She raised an eyebrow. 'You're saying I've got bags under my eyes?'

He flapped a dismissive hand. 'No. I'm saying usually your irises are the soft grey of an autumn mist. But when you're upset or angry about something, there's a dark ring round the outer edge. Like storm clouds coming in.'

'Very poetic, Dr Gallagher.' But she was amazed that he'd noticed such a tiny detail.

'So what's wrong?'

She grimaced. 'It's going to sound childish.'

'Tell me anyway.'

She took a deep breath. 'OK. I feel as if you're ignoring me at work.'

He frowned. 'Of course I'm not. We work together. I think we're a pretty good team, actually.'

'But you never suggest going for coffee or lunch.'

'Ah. *That* sort of ignoring.' He stole a kiss. 'We agreed we're trying to stay under the radar of the hospital grapevine.'

'That's a mixed metaphor.'

'I don't care.' He drew her close. 'Abby. If people at work know we're together, we're just going to get hassled. Everyone's going to tell me that you're too good for me, and everyone's going to tell you that I break hearts on a daily basis.'

She sighed. 'I know.' And she could really understand now why Lewis had a reputation as a heartbreaker. She had a nasty feeling that he could break hers.

'It doesn't change things between you and me. But it means we get to explore wherever this is going without any hassle.'

'Uh-huh.' She still wasn't entirely convinced.

He kissed her. 'Trust me, this really is the best way.'

Trust. That was the rub. It was the thing she found hardest. But if this thing between them was going to work, she'd just have to try.

'Let's go and finish watching your film. We need two spoons.'

'And bowls.'

'No. It's more fun to eat straight from the tub.' He gave her a wicked grin. 'If I'm greedy and scoff more than my share, you can make me do a forfeit. I'll do anything you ask.'

Oh, the thoughts that put in her head. Totally wanton. And she blushed to the roots of her hair. That was something else new that Lewis had brought out in her. She definitely hadn't had sex on the brain before meeting him.

'I love it when you do that.'

'Do what?'

He kissed her. 'Blush. You're so cute.'

She wrinkled her nose. 'It clashes with my hair.'

'No.' He took the scrunchie out of her hair and twirled a lock of hair round his fingers. 'I love your hair. I know you're sensible and wear it up at work, but it's glorious down. Definitely the mermaid look.'

She couldn't stay annoyed with him. Not when he was being playful and sweet. She fetched two spoons and curled up on the sofa with him. Though she couldn't concentrate on the rest of the film, not with Lewis so near. She was too aware of him. Of the warmth of his body, the citrusy tang of his aftershave, the muscular feel of his arms wrapped round her.

'I'm sorry. I didn't mean to spoil your evening,' he said as the credits rolled.

'You didn't. The film wasn't as good as I thought it would be.' She shifted so she was facing him and laid her palm against his cheek. 'And you were bored, weren't you?'

'Rom-coms aren't really my thing,' he agreed. He twisted slightly so he could kiss her palm. 'I like a good action movie.'

'Now, why doesn't that surprise me, coming from an adrenalin fiend?' she teased.

'If it walks like a duck and quacks like a duck…' he said, spreading his hands.

She laughed, and kissed him. 'Were you an adrenalin fiend when you were growing up?'

* * *

'I guess so. I used to climb trees and roller-skate too fast down slopes.' At least, until he'd been fourteen. Then he'd had to learn to be domesticated. Fast.

'What about your sisters? Are they adrenalin fiends, too?'

'No, they're girly. Well, Dani and Ronnie have fairly big nerdy streaks,' he amended. 'Manda's your typical drama teacher, with floaty scarves and lots of hats—oh, and her hair colour never stays the same two months running.'

'It must've been fun growing up in your house,' she said wistfully.

'It was.' Until his dad had died and life had turned upside down. 'Noisy, though. And sometimes it was hard to find a corner of space just for you. I guess that's part of why I like doing the outdoor stuff. It gave me space.'

'Were your parents outdoor types?'

'Dad was. He was in the local mountain rescue team. I guess that's what sparked my interest in the first place—I wanted to follow in his footsteps.'

'Did you?'

He nodded. 'I used to hang around the team and help with the communications bit when I was smaller, then when I was old enough I did the training and I became part of the team.' Not until after his dad had died, but the team had taken pity on him and let him start a bit younger. They'd understood why he'd needed to do it.

'You miss it, don't you?'

'Yes. I did think about going back to the Peak district and working in the nearest emergency department, so I could work with the mountain rescue team again.'

Which was something he'd never told anyone. Why was he spilling his guts to Abigail? He needed to shut up. Now.

'Why don't you?'

Because it was complicated. And he wasn't ready to explain about his mother. 'I like living in London,' he said simply. 'And I can still do outdoor stuff here.'

'Like zip-lining and skydiving.'

'You enjoyed it, too,' he pointed out.

She smiled. 'Yes. But I don't think I could keep up with your pace.'

'Hey. We're having a quiet evening in front of the television, are we not?'

'And you're bored.'

'I'm not bored with your company,' he said softly. And he spent the next half an hour proving it, to their mutual satisfaction.

Friday night was the team ice-skating night. Abigail discovered that, just as Marina had said, Max was good at skating. Marco was on duty, or no doubt he would've been doing a double act with Max, but Sydney spent more time falling over than skating—and so did Abigail. And Lewis, just as she'd suspected, turned out to be brilliant.

'OK, you two. I can't stand by and see you do this any more. I'm going to teach you to skate. Sydney, you first,' Lewis directed. 'You're not going to fall because I won't let you, so stop over-thinking it.'

He proceeded to coax her round the edge of the rink, holding her hand and directing her movements. Abigail watched them and could see Sydney relaxing, becoming more confident and skating more smoothly as Lewis coached her.

Right at that moment she could see why Lewis had taken a gap-year job with a training company. He was a natural teacher, using the same skills he used as a doctor: calmness, patience and precision.

'Marco's never going to believe this,' Sydney said as she came to a halt by Abigail.

'I'll vouch for you if he asks. Sorry, I should've thought to film you on my phone. It looked pretty good from here.'

'I can skate. I can actually *skate*.' Sydney beamed at her. 'Abby, you have to let him teach you next. It's amazing.'

Lewis held out his hand. 'Your turn, then, Abby. And stop panicking. You saw Sydney do it. I'm not going to let you fall either.'

'Trust you, you're a doctor?' Abigail asked wryly.

He laughed. 'Something like that. Come on.' He lowered his voice as they moved away from the others in the team. 'And it's a great excuse for me to hold your hand in public without anyone asking questions.'

She couldn't help it. She blushed to the roots of her hair.

He smiled. 'If half the emergency department wasn't on the rink, I'd kiss you. Because you look adorable. But that'll have to wait until later.' He drew her just a little bit closer. 'And I'm really going to enjoy paying up on that particular promise.'

He slowly guided her round the rink, praising her as her confidence grew and correcting her technique without being bossy. And then she was skating. Gliding across the ice—holding Lewis's hand, admittedly, but not clutching the handrail, almost too terrified to move.

'I feel like a swan. Or a mermaid.'

'Mermaid on ice. That's a new one.' He smiled. 'We'll have to come to the rink again. Just the two of us.'

'I'd like that.'

'Look at you two,' Marina said as she skated up to them. 'You look like the perfect couple.'

Abigail felt the panic seep through her. Did Marina know, or was she just teasing? Abigail couldn't really read her friend's expression. 'I'm just his project,' she said. 'And did you see him teach Syd to skate?'

Marina smiled. 'He's a real Sir Galahad at heart, our Lewis.'

Lewis, predictably, did a twirl on the ice and then bowed. 'Thank you, kind madam.'

'Oh, you.' Marina laughed, and skated back to Max, greeting him with a kiss.

'You were brilliant. And I filmed you skating so you can see for yourself,' Sydney said when they returned to where they'd left her. She handed over her mobile phone. 'Take a look.'

Their heads were actually touching as they reviewed the footage. And Abigail had a nasty feeling that Marina hadn't been teasing. Because they *did* look like a couple. The way they smiled at each other, exchanged little glances—the tender expression on Lewis's face. Oh, help. How was Lewis, Mr Three-Dates-and-You're-Out, going to see all this?

Lewis wasn't prepared for the footage. The way Abigail looked at him, her expression all soft and trusting instead of the slightly wary look the doctor he'd first met had worn. Marina had been teasing—of course she had—but at the same time she had a point. They *did* look like a couple. Which was crazy, because they both had issues and neither of them wanted to settle down.

What if...?

He shook himself mentally. 'Ten out of ten for effort, Abby. You, too, Syd,' he said.

'I don't think we should tell you how good you are, Lewis, or your head will swell so much you'll never get through the doorway,' Sydney teased back.

He just laughed. 'So did you both enjoy it?'

'Definitely,' Abigail said. 'If anyone had told me last week that I'd be skating in the middle of the rink, I would never have believed them. I'm way too clumsy.'

'All it takes is practice,' Lewis said.

When their slot at the rink was over, the team headed for the pizza parlour, where Marina had booked their table. Somehow Lewis managed to sit next to Abigail; he held her hand briefly under the table, making her feel warm all over. When their pizzas arrived, he pinched two of the artichoke hearts off her pizza.

'It's payment for teaching you to skate,' he claimed at her pained look.

'You haven't taken anything from Sydney's pizza,' she pointed out.

'That's because she's sitting at the other end of the table.' He winked at her. 'But I can tell you that her secret chocolate stash is going to be under major threat next week. I know where she keeps it.'

'You're impossible,' Abigail said, rolling her eyes.

But she absolutely loved the team evening out. For

the first time she could remember she actually felt part of things. Valued for who she was. It was a weird feeling, but one she wanted to get used to.

At the end of the meal, Lewis said, 'Abby, you're on the same Tube line as me, aren't you? I'll walk you to the station.'

Nobody batted an eyelid or seemed to take his words as anything other than a colleague being gallant, so she smiled. 'Thanks.'

He didn't hold her hand or kiss her after they left the restaurant, and Abigail guessed why—in case someone came out into the street and saw them. But as soon as they were on the train and were sure they didn't know anyone else in the carriage, Lewis hauled her onto his lap.

'Lewis, you can't do this sort of thing on the Tu—' she began.

He kissed her words away. 'Yes, we can. I've been dying to hold you properly all night, and I can't wait any longer.'

It was the same for her, so she could hardly protest.

And he held her hand all the way from the Tube station to her flat.

'Do you want to come in for coffee?' she asked.

'Decaf, please,' he said.

She bustled about the kitchen, making coffee. 'I had a wonderful evening. Thanks for teaching me to skate.'

He smiled. 'Pleasure.'

'Is there anything you're not good at?'

He pretended to think about it. 'Well, I can't knit or crochet.'

She cuffed his arm lightly. 'You know what I mean. You're good at everything.'

'Everything? Why, thank you, ma'am,' he drawled. Her blush made his grin broaden. 'But I could always do with some practice…'

He started kissing her, and the coffee was forgotten as he carried her to her bed.

Afterwards, Abigail was half tempted to ask him to stay the night, but she knew he'd back away. Given his commitment phobia, no doubt he had a few mental adjustments to make about their fling, too. Maybe it would be better to just enjoy this while it lasted and not expect too much.

'I have to go,' he said, pulling his clothes back on. 'Stay there. You look comfortable. I can see myself out.'

She nodded. 'See you at work.'

He leaned over to kiss her. 'Sweet dreams.'

'You, too.' She kissed him back.

Was she doing the right thing, having a fling with Lewis? she wondered as she heard the front door close behind him. She'd had such a good time tonight, really feeling part of the crowd. And she knew she had Lewis to thank for that. Knowing he was there had given her confidence and helped her feel comfortable in a group setting.

Their fling didn't have a stated time limit, though she knew it would end between them because Lewis had made it clear that he didn't want to be tied down. But fear bubbled through her at the idea of it ending.

Lewis was the one who was responsible for her fitting in on the team night out. How would she manage without that safety net? And, given that Lewis was a party boy who'd never miss a team night out, what would that mean for her if things got awkward after their break-up and she had to avoid him? Would she end up back in her old lonely life, trapped by her lack of social skills?

Worse still was the fear that her feelings were already starting to run away with her where Lewis was concerned. Somehow she was going to have to get them back under control. Lewis wouldn't change, and she couldn't let herself hope for more than he was able to offer. That wouldn't be fair to either of them.

She groaned and rolled over in bed. On the side that was still warm from Lewis's body heat. 'Cinnamon Abigail Brydon Smith, you really need to stop over-analysing this and get a grip,' she told herself crossly. 'It's a fling. Probably for more than just three dates, but still only a fling. Just enjoy it for what it is and don't be so sad and needy.'

Which was easier said than done.

CHAPTER EIGHT

OVER THE NEXT few weeks Abigail got used to her double life, being just colleagues with Lewis at work and lovers outside. She enjoyed spending time with him, a mix of doing the adrenalin-fiend stuff he loved and the gentler, quieter stuff she was used to doing in her spare time. And they were quietly synchronising their off-duty days so they could spend more of their days off together. Nobody in the department had commented, so they were definitely getting away with it, Abigail thought.

'So where exactly are we going?' Lewis asked when he met her at her flat on the Thursday morning.

'Somewhere I really like. You might find it boring—or you might not. And we can walk there from here,' she said.

'An art gallery?' he asked when they arrived, sounding surprised.

'Keep an open mind,' she said.

Inside, she led him through the maze of rooms to the one containing her favourite paintings. 'This is where I like to come on a wet afternoon. I love these paintings and the colours.'

'They're very bright, considering they must be a hundred years old.'

'A hundred and fifty,' she corrected him. 'That's because they used to paint on a wet white background, a bit like the old fresco painters.'

Lewis smiled. 'Your nerdy streak's coming out, princess.'

She closed her eyes. 'Sorry. I'm being boring. I'll shut up now.'

'No—you're all animated when you talk about the paintings, and I like seeing you like this.' He wandered round with her, hand in hand, examining the paintings.

'It's not like seeing a print or a postcard. The real things are totally different. Take this one.' She pointed out a painting by Millais. 'A print makes the model's clothes look flat and a bit boring. But if you look at the real thing up close, you can see they're actually iridescent.'

He peered at it. 'You're right. How do you know this sort of thing?'

'Because I always had my head in a book when I was a kid—probably while you were outside climbing trees,' she added wryly.

'Probably,' he agreed. 'My sisters would like you.'

Maybe, she thought, but you haven't asked me to meet them. Then again, she hadn't asked him to meet her father either, so she wasn't in a position to complain.

They walked over to look at the next painting. 'Now, this one reminds me of you,' he said.

'Rossetti's *Lady Lilith*?' she asked, surprised.

'Uh-huh. Combing your glorious hair in a bower of roses.'

She raised an eyebrow. 'Considering my hair's dead straight and the model has curls...' Like she'd had years ago. Cinnamon baby. As she'd grown older, her hair had straightened. Dull and boring, like she was herself.

'It's a similar colour, like copper in sunlight. And a similar length.' He stood behind her with his arms wrapped round her waist and rested his cheek against her hair. 'And your hair smells of roses. I rest my case.'

If anyone had said to Lewis that he'd enjoy wandering around an art gallery, he would've scoffed; he'd always thought them a bit dull and he would much rather have been doing something active. But with Abigail he really enjoyed it. She made him look at things differently.

Which in itself was scary. He'd promised himself that he wouldn't get involved with her, wouldn't let himself get too close, because he knew from experience that you just couldn't have it all. The trouble was, Abigail Smith made him want to take that risk.

He shook himself, not wanting to spoil his day with her, and concentrated on the paintings. They took a break for coffee and cake, then browsed in the shop. He saw a fridge magnet of the painting that reminded him of her and couldn't resist buying it.

'So now we get to do some adrenalin-fiend stuff?' he asked.

She shook her head. 'It's still my day. We're doing staid, quiet, nerdy stuff.'

'You're not even going to give a clue about what we're going to do?' he grumbled.

'You mean, like you did when you planned to chuck me out of a plane?'

But there was a sparkle in her eyes, so he knew she wasn't really cross about it. 'That was a controlled descent, princess, and you were strapped to me.'

'OK. What we're doing is on the other side of the Thames.'

Which told him next to nothing. He didn't manage to kiss any more information out of her either.

But when they reached the station at Blackfriars and she shepherded him across the Millennium footbridge, he had a pretty good idea of what she had in mind. 'Another art gallery,' he said, looking up at the enormous chimney of the brick building in front of them. And this time it was modern art. Which he really didn't get. He only hoped that she didn't want to spend the rest of the afternoon doing something so tedious, because he'd get seriously itchy feet.

She laughed. 'Don't look so worried. I realise I've art-galleried you out for today. No, I have something else in mind. We're heading this way.'

As soon as he saw the white, timber-framed, polygonal building with its thatched roof, he knew. 'Shakespeare,' he said with a smile. 'Now we're back on more normal territory for me.'

'Oh, of course—your sister's a drama teacher. I take it you've been here with her?' she asked.

'I've been a few times, yes. Enough to know to rent a cushion to sit on.' He smiled at her. 'I assume we have seats? I can't quite see you doing the groundling thing and standing in the yard.'

'And getting either too hot or too wet? No. I'd rather sit under cover. And me, too, on the cushions. I learned that one the hard way, too. Literally, on those benches,' she said with a smile.

The matinée performance turned out to be *Much Ado About Nothing*.

'The original rom-com,' she said with an arch look.

'Ah, but I like this one. And it has some action scenes as well as the mushy stuff, so I'm happy,' he said, squeezing her shoulders briefly and kissing the top of her head.

He held her hand through the whole performance. And he couldn't help tightening his fingers round hers when Benedick said to Beatrice, 'I do love nothing in the world so well as you. Is that not strange?'

Was he beginning to fall in love with Abigail?

He shook himself. Of course not. He was way too sensible to let his heart get involved. He was just letting the romance of the play get to him—especially as they were seeing it only a few hundred yards away from where Shakespeare's company had performed the play, in a building that was as near as you could get to the original.

They walked along the bank of the Thames afterwards, enjoying the late afternoon sunshine, and eventually found a small Moroccan restaurant. This time he joined her in choosing a rich vegetable tagine and then cinnamon-spiced oranges served with tiny almond-studded biscuits.

Sitting on a low cushion opposite him, with the tiny tealight candles making her hair seem all shades of bronze and copper, she looked utterly beautiful. Funny, a day of doing quiet things should've left him with itchy feet, desperate to go and do something so he didn't have to think or let any emotions run riot in his head. But, weirdly, he could be quiet with Abigail. And he found himself lingering over the meal. Just being with her was enough.

Back at Abigail's flat, Lewis kissed her goodnight on the doorstep. He was tempted to ask if he could stay, and that scared him. He hadn't felt like that about any-one in years.

'You're on an early shift tomorrow, aren't you?' he asked.

She nodded.

'Then I'd better go and let you get some sleep.'

She looked faintly disappointed, as if she'd been about to ask him in for coffee.

'But thank you for today,' he said hastily. 'I really enjoyed it.'

'Even though it wasn't adrenalin-fiend stuff?'

'Actually, yes.' He had to be honest. 'I couldn't have done a second art gallery, but I enjoyed the play. And dinner.' And being with her. 'I'll see you later.' He kissed her again, and left.

But he couldn't settle, back at his flat. That feeling, earlier, that he might be falling in love with Abigail… It couldn't happen. Long term didn't work for him; he'd been a total mess after Jenna. Of course he knew that Abigail wasn't like Jenna, but he still wasn't prepared to take any risks. His life was on an even keel now and he wanted it to stay that way. Light and fun and not hav-ing to think about anything emotional.

He ended up putting his running shoes on and going out. It didn't matter that it had started to drizzle. He needed to move, to get the adrenalin and endorphins flowing. To drown out everything that was in his head.

It took Lewis a week to risk seeing Abigail again out-side work. 'Can you swap with someone so you're off on Tuesday?' he asked.

'Probably. Why?'

'Because I want to take you somewhere.'

'And wear sensible shoes?' she asked wryly.

'I don't say that all the time.'

She laughed. 'Yes, you do. Even though you know I don't own anything apart from sensible shoes.'

He let that pass. 'Do you have such a thing as a floaty dress?'

'I'm not *that* ungirly, Lewis.'

He leaned forward and kissed her. 'You're girly enough for me.' Oh, now, why had he said that? Hinting at a promise he knew full well he wouldn't be able to keep. It wasn't fair to either of them. He should just stay away from her.

But he couldn't. She drew him like nobody else ever had. And he couldn't work out why. Why was he drawn to a quiet, shy, clever woman who had no confidence in herself? Why was he drawn to someone who was the complete opposite of the party-loving women he usually dated?

'Wear your dress next Tuesday,' he said. 'I'll meet you at your flat at eleven.'

Her black and white floaty dress was perfect for what he had in mind. But the shoes weren't. They were low-heeled and black, reminding him of ballet pumps. And for this she needed heels. And, he thought, some colour.

'Are all your shoes low-heeled and black?' he asked.

'Yes.' She lifted her chin. 'Is there a problem?'

'Nothing I can't fix.'

She frowned. 'What are we doing?'

'It's a surprise. And, no, it doesn't involve skydiving, zip-lining or swimming with sharks.'

Her eyes widened. 'I hope that last bit was a joke and you're not planning that at some point in the future.'

'Why? Wouldn't you like to swim with sharks?'

'I'll pass on that one, I think. Dolphins, maybe—but not sharks. Too many teeth.'

'Chicken.' He laughed. 'Come on. Let's go.' He took her to Covent Garden.

'Oh, are we having lunch?' Her face cleared. 'So that's why you wanted me to wear a floaty dress. To look girly for once.'

'Nope. We can stop for a sandwich if we're quick, but we're here to go shopping.'

'For what?'

He was going to have to tell her now. 'To get you some dancing shoes.'

'Dancing shoes?' she repeated. 'Why?'

'Because we're going dancing.'

'But—how? The nightclubs aren't open in the afternoon.'

'I didn't say we were going clubbing. We're going *dancing.*'

Abigail had no idea where Lewis was planning to take her dancing, especially at this time of day. But she'd enjoyed the other mad activities he'd introduced her to, so she decided to go with it.

'I would've liked to have done this as a surprise,' he said, 'but you really can't buy someone a pair of shoes as a surprise. Not if you want them to fit properly.'

She remembered what he'd once said about wanting to see her wearing nothing but a pair of high heels and went hot all over. To cover the fact that she was flustered, she said, 'But I can't dance.'

'You don't need to,' he said with a smile. 'Just let me lead.'

She gave him a speaking look, and he laughed. 'You really have problems trusting people, don't you?'

She lifted her chin and told an outright fib. 'No.'

'It's going to be fun. I promise.' He led her into a shop. 'As you said yourself, you don't totter around on high heels every day, so it'll be easier for you to get a pair with a medium heel.'

'Why do my shoes need a heel at all?'

'Because it makes it easier for you to dance in. And, no, the shoes you're wearing aren't going to work as dancing shoes.'

She couldn't resist a pair of purple satin shoes with diamante buckles, but she refused to let him buy them for her. 'I'm perfectly capable of buying my own shoes.'

'There weren't any strings attached, princess,' he said softly. 'I just wanted to do something nice for you.'

And then she felt mean. How did Lewis manage to wrong-foot her so often?

'Don't go prickly on me, Abby. We're going to have fun. Really.'

'I know. I'm sorry.'

He stroked her cheek. 'You really have been dating the wrong sort of men.'

'Mmm.' She didn't want to think about that.

He took her to a hotel in the West End. She looked at him, puzzled, as they stood outside. 'I thought you said we were going dancing?'

'We are, and this used to be one of the most popular venues in London for dances years ago. They have regular tea dances here.'

'Tea dances?'

'Ballroom dancing and cups of tea,' he explained. 'In very nice porcelain cups.'

This was absolutely the last thing she'd expected. She shook her head in bemusement. 'You never fail to surprise me, Lewis. Where did you learn to dance?'

He shrugged. 'It doesn't matter.'

'Is this something to do with the training company you worked for?'

'No.'

'A way to get the girls at med school?'

He laughed. 'No. All right, if you really want to know, I had a patient who broke her hip. I spent some time with her while we were waiting for a slot in Theatre.'

In other words, she thought, the old lady didn't have anyone to wait with her, and Lewis had given up his break to wait with her and make sure that she wasn't frightened and alone. Abigail was coming to recognise that he did that sort of thing a lot. Without any fuss, without drawing attention to himself, he just saw something that needed to be fixed and did it.

'And she liked dancing?'

'When she was younger, yes—she told me a lot about it. And she said I reminded her of her son.' He grimaced. 'It turned out her son was a soldier, and he'd been killed on duty. Her husband had died years before so she was completely alone. And I promised her that, when her hip was fixed, I'd take her dancing.'

Abigail had a pretty good idea that Lewis had done a lot more than that. That he'd visited the old lady and that he'd made sure she was being looked after properly. 'So you took lessons?'

He nodded. 'I promised her a waltz. We came here because she used to dance here with her husband. We were going to make it a regular thing and come here once a month.'

'But?' she asked softly.

'She caught pneumonia before we could come again. And, she, um, didn't make it back here with me.'

She held him close. 'I'm sorry.'

'Me, too. But I did manage to bring back some good memories for her. And I discovered I liked this kind of dancing.'

'I take it Marina doesn't know about this or she would've got you to offer a dancing lesson for the auction.'

'No. It was at my last hospital. I was still a wet-behind-the-ears, very junior doctor.'

She sighed. 'I really don't get why you let people think you're a selfish heartbreaker, Lewis. You're a good man.'

He shrugged, and kissed her.

Which told her that he really didn't want to talk about it. She was definitely going to have to resort to that poker game to get him to open up to her.

'You need to change your shoes here and check your bag into the cloakroom,' he said, and waited for her to do it.

It felt odd wearing such girly shoes; and here, at the hotel, they looked much brighter than they had in the shop. She wished that she'd bought something more invisible. Something to let her fade into the background like she normally did.

'Don't look so worried. I promise not to stand on your toes.'

'I'm not worried about that.'

He took her hand and squeezed it. 'This doesn't have

to be complicated. We can make it as simple and easy as you want. The idea is just to have fun.'

Fun. That was what made Lewis tick.

But she was pretty sure there was more to it than that. She had a feeling that Lewis kept himself busy doing physical things that needed concentration and meant that you didn't have time to think.

'Oh, and wear your hair down.'

She wrinkled her nose. 'It gets in the way.'

'I love your hair,' he said simply, reaching out to twirl the ends round his fingers.

She gave in and let him remove the hair band, then walked with him into the room where the tea dance was being held.

It was amazing. The roof was curved glass, letting so much light into the room. There were tables dotted round the outside, waiters and waitresses in traditional black and white uniforms carrying trays of tea and cakes, and more palm trees than she'd ever seen before in her life. And the floor was packed, she noticed, with couples of all ages.

'The tea dances are pretty popular,' Lewis said, as if reading her mind.

People were practising before the music started. She watched them, fascinated. 'Lewis, I hope you realise I don't have a clue how to do that sort of thing.'

'Have you ever been to an aerobics class?' he asked.

'Yes.'

'So you can follow a small routine.'

'Well, once I've learned the steps.'

'OK. Here's the cha cha cha.' He stood facing her. 'Your left hand goes here...' he put it in position on his arm '...and you hold my right hand.'

So far, so good, she thought.

'Now, your right foot goes back.' He moved forward with his right foot, and she found herself stepping back automatically.

'Good. Now, keep your weight on the back foot, then shift the weight forward again.' The pressure of his palm on her back led her to copy his movements.

'And now it's the cha cha cha bit—you take a small step to the side with your right foot, bring your left to join it, and a small step to the right again.' Again, he led her through it.

'And that's it?'

'Then we do it back the other way. Think of it as rock, rock, side to side.' He led her through it. 'And we can add some twirly bits onto it when you're confident with that. We'll take it at your pace, no rush.'

The band struck up the first number.

'This is a quickstep, so it's probably not fair to start you on this. Let's sit this one out and watch.' He found a chair and settled her on his lap as he sat down.

She felt her eyes widen. 'Lewis, we can't do this.'

'Nobody's watching us. They're either watching the dancers or they're too busy dancing to notice what anyone else is doing,' he soothed. 'Be with me and just enjoy it.'

Something about his nearness calmed her, and she found herself enjoying the music—even though it wasn't the kind of thing she usually listened to and definitely wasn't the sort of thing she thought Lewis would like.

Then the band played a different song and he gently moved her off his lap and led her on to the dance floor. 'Time to cha cha cha, princess.'

She was expecting to be stumbling all over the place

but Lewis kept her close, pointing her in the right direction all the time. Having seen what other people were doing, she had the confidence to let him talk her through a twirly bit—and then realised that she was really enjoying herself.

'See?' He leant over and stole a kiss. 'It's fun.'

'Yes, it is.' She smiled at him. 'I've never done anything like this before. I tended to avoid the dances at university.'

'If yours were like the ones I went to, they weren't exactly dances—just people moving awkwardly about, out of time with the music, and spotty teenage students hoping that someone might let them grope them in the dark.'

'I can't imagine you being a spotty teenage student,' she teased.

For a moment she thought she saw a flash of panic in his eyes.

Then he laughed. 'Are you saying I'm vain?'

'No, I just don't think you would've ever been one of the desperate ones.'

'I'll take that as a compliment, even though I think there's an edge to it.'

'No edge,' she said. 'But you have to know you're beautiful, Lewis. Women look at you all the time.'

He shrugged. 'I'm just me.'

She laughed. 'You're blushing.'

He kissed her—a move she was beginning to realise he used to stop a conversation that made him feel uncomfortable. So much like Benedick, in the play they'd seen together. *'I'll stop your mouth...'* Lewis had held her hand particularly tightly during that line. And another, which half made her wonder...

The song ended and the next one began. She recognised the timing as a three-four beat—the sort her father used when he wrote a ballad.

'This is a waltz,' Lewis said. 'We're not going to do anything flashy with it today, just the basic steps. I'll teach you the twirly bits another time.'

'OK.'

'Just go where I lead you. Try and remember it's alternate legs, and it goes back, side, together then forward, side, together.'

He was asking a lot, she thought. And his idea of fun definitely meant that you didn't have time to do anything except concentrate on your physical movements.

But then he started dancing with her, and it turned out to be a lot easier than she'd expected. He talked her through the steps as they went round the room, but at the same time he was guiding her so she didn't go wrong. She let herself relax and enjoy it.

The first few numbers were instrumental, but then a woman with a smoky jazz-style voice came to join the orchestra. Abigail thoroughly enjoyed doing the fast cha cha chas with him and then slowing it down again for the waltz, held close in his arms all the time. Now she knew why he'd asked her to wear a floaty dress. And he was right about the shoes, too.

At that moment she actually felt like the princess he teased her about being. Except she wasn't made of ice. With Lewis, she was all flame.

The afternoon seemed to just vanish, and she was disappointed when the orchestra had played their last number.

'Thank you—I really enjoyed this,' she said. She kissed him impulsively. 'Can we do it again?'

'They hold tea dances once a month. I can get us tickets for the next one, if you like.'

'That'd be great. It's my turn to pay, though.'

He raised an eyebrow. 'If you insist.'

'I do.'

She retrieved her bag from the cloakroom, changed her shoes, and they caught the Tube back to his flat.

'I forgot to tell you—you look lovely in that dress.' He kissed her lightly. 'Dance with me again?'

How could she resist? She changed into her dancing shoes while he put some music on. And although she'd enjoyed the faster dance, she was glad that he chose a waltz, where he could hold her closer.

Somehow they ended up dancing down the corridor from the living room to Lewis's bedroom. And somehow he managed to peel off her dress while they were dancing, leaving her in just her underwear and the dance shoes.

He dragged in a breath. 'Abigail Smith, you're the most gorgeous woman I've ever seen. Do you have any idea what you do to me?'

Shyness flooded through her but he held her hands. 'Don't cover yourself up, princess. I meant it. You're gorgeous.' He lifted one hand above her head, and she found herself doing the pirouette he'd taught her on the dance floor. 'Every inch of you is lovely,' he said softly. 'Every inch of you makes me want to touch you and taste you. And those shoes make your legs look as if they go on for ever.'

The intensity of his gaze told her that he wasn't just spinning her a line. He really was that attracted to her.

A slow burn of desire fizzled through her as he kissed her and finished undressing her.

Finally, he knelt at her feet and removed her shoes.

He looked up at her then, and that smile was just for her. A smile that made her heart feel as if it had done a backflip. A feeling she'd had about nobody else.

She realised then that she'd just broken every single rule and fallen for Lewis. A man who'd pushed her way out of her comfort zone and made her realise that she could do so much more than she thought she could. A man who'd taught her to trust again, even though he didn't do commitment and had made no promises for the future to her.

Totally crazy. This could only end in tears, and she should back off.

But then she stopped thinking as he stripped off his own clothing then scooped her up and laid her back against his pillows. And as he eased into her body, she couldn't help feeling that there had to be a way to make this turn out all right. They were good together. They had fun—and yet there was more to it than that. A connection like she'd never felt with anyone else.

If she just could get him to open up to her, if they could be honest about who they were—then maybe, just maybe, this would turn out all right. For both of them.

CHAPTER NINE

ABIGAIL WAS ROSTERED in Resus the next morning, while Lewis was in Minors. Her second patient of the morning was a serious one.

Biddy, one of the paramedics, came in to do the handover. 'This is Matthew. He's fifty-five. He's been diagnosed with flu by his family doctor and he hasn't been able to get his temperature down for a couple of days—at the moment it's thirty-nine degrees C but he's still feeling cold.'

Abigail had noticed the violent shivering. And it wasn't a good sign.

'He tried to get out of bed this morning to get himself a drink, but he thought he was going to pass out. He called his wife, who was at work,' Biddy said. 'She called us and she's on her way in now.'

'Thanks, Biddy. What are his obs?' Abigail asked.

'His heartbeat and respiration are both a bit too fast for my liking, and he's been a bit confused on the way in.'

It *could* be flu, Abigail thought. But when she laid her hand on Matthew's to give it a reassuring squeeze, she noticed his skin was cold, clammy and pale. No, this wasn't a simple case of flu. This had progressed a stage further.

'Thanks for your help, Biddy,' she said.

'No worries. But my gut tells me it's not just flu.'

'I agree.' She looked at Dawn, the nurse who'd been rostered with her. 'I think we're looking at sepsis—the flu's making his body shut down. I want to put him on antibiotics straight away.'

The paramedic team had already put a line in so Abigail gave Matthew some high-flow oxygen while Dawn took blood samples and then gave him some broad-spectrum antibiotics and put him on a drip to help with dehydration.

'We need to monitor his urine output,' she said to Dawn.

The nurse nodded. 'I'll get the catheter kit.'

Abigail had just finished inserting the catheter and making Matthew comfortable when an anxious-looking woman came in with the triage nurse. 'I think my husband's here? Matthew?'

'Yes. I'm Abby Smith and I'm looking after him today.'

'I'm Bella.' The woman bit her lip. 'What's happening? I thought he had flu, and I left him in bed—but then he rang me and said he felt really ill and thought he was going to pass out. I called the ambulance.'

'Which was exactly the right thing to do,' Abigail reassured her.

'So is it not flu, then?'

'Sometimes the body's immune system overreacts to an illness like flu and causes sepsis,' Abigail explained, 'and that's what Matthew's symptoms are telling me.'

'Sepsis?' Bella frowned. 'Is that like blood poisoning?'

'It used to be called that, yes. Basically the body deals with infection by producing white blood cells, which cause inflammation around the infection and stops it spreading. With sepsis, the inflammation spreads throughout the body. That's why Matthew's got a temperature and his heartbeat and breathing are a bit on the fast side.'

'Is he going to be all right?' Bella asked.

Abigail's heart sank. She knew that with cases of sepsis a third to a half of patients didn't make it. Had they started treatment in time for Matthew to get through it? 'We're doing our best,' she said gently. 'At the moment we're giving him antibiotics and keeping a very close eye on him. But if the infection starts to affect his organs, we might need to send him to Intensive Care so his breathing and circulation can be supported while we treat the infection.'

Bella looked terrified. 'Can I stay with him?'

'Of course you can, and if you've got any questions just ask me. I'm not too busy and it doesn't matter if you think the questions are little and unimportant—you need to know what's going on.'

However, over the next couple of hours Matthew's condition worsened.

Abigail sat down with Matthew's wife. 'Bella, I'm going to send him up to Intensive Care. I know even the department name is scary, but the staff are great and they can look after him better than we can down here,' she said.

She went up to Intensive Care with Bella and Matthew so she could do the handover, introduce Bella to the staff and help them settle in. And she spent her lunch break there, too. She knew Bella wouldn't want to leave Matthew's side so she brought up some cheese sandwiches and a bottle of water.

Bella's eyes filled with tears. 'That's so kind. Thank you.'

'It's the least I can do. I know how I'd feel in your shoes.' If she was at her father's bedside, she'd be frantic and not want to leave for a second. 'I can get you a hot drink, too—just let me know what you'd like.'

'No, this is fine.'

'Make sure you eat them,' Abigail said. 'I know you're worried about Matthew, but you need to look after yourself, too.'

Throughout the day Abigail wondered how Matthew was doing. But then, an hour before the end of her shift, Bella came down to see her. 'Abby? I just wanted to let you know that Matthew...' her breath hitched '...passed away.' She swallowed hard. 'And I wanted to say thank you, because you were so kind earlier.'

Abigail blew out a breath. He hadn't made it. 'I'm so sorry.'

'I've got to tell the kids. I sent them a text to say their dad wasn't well so go to their grandmother's after school and I'll collect them later.' She shook her head. 'I can't believe he's gone.'

At a loss for words, Abigail hugged her. Bella gave a small sob then straightened her back. 'I'd better go and call the kids. But thank you for what you did. I know you did your best for Matthew.'

Yes, but it wasn't good enough, was it? Abigail thought. Not nearly good enough.

Dully, she watched Bella leave the department, then headed to find Dawn to let her know before going to the staff kitchen and putting the kettle on. Right now she needed some hot, sweet tea. And she felt sick. She'd just lost somebody's dad. She knew it was ridiculous to be superstitious, but she couldn't help thinking that what goes around comes around. Please don't let there be karma and let her lose her father, too.

Unable to settle even after drinking half the tea, she called him. 'Dad?'

'Hello, darling. I thought you were at work. Is everything all right?'

'I, um, just lost a patient. Sorry, I'm being horribly wet. I just wanted to—well—talk to you.' Her voice gave a treacherous wobble.

'Cinnamon, stay right where you are and I'll come and get you.'

'No, don't do that. I've still got a bit of my shift to go. It's not fair on the others if I just walk out.' She sniffed. 'I know I'm being stupid. But I just wanted to tell you I love you.'

'I love you, too, darling.' He sighed. 'I wish I could wave a magic wand for you.'

'Right now I could really do with one of those. I might've been able to save my patient.'

'It wasn't your fault. You did your best, and nobody could ask any more of you.'

Keith was the one person in her life who'd always, always believed in her. Who'd been there for her—unlike her mother. 'Sorry, Dad. I know you're probably busy. I'm sorry if I just took stuff out of your head.'

'My person from Porlock, you mean?' He laughed. 'I'm never too busy for you, Cinnamon, and don't you ever think I will be, because I won't.'

'I know, Dad.' He'd always made time for her. Even

when it hadn't really been convenient for him. 'I'd better get back to work. I'll call you tomorrow.'

'Better than that, I'll take you out for dinner. I'll book somewhere and I'll meet you at your flat at, what, seven?'

She smiled. 'I'd like that. See you tomorrow.'

'Love you.'

'Love you, too.'

When she ended the call, she realised that Lewis had walked into the kitchen.

'I take it that was your dad?' he asked.

She frowned. 'Why do you think that?'

'Because, according to Dawn, you just lost a middle-aged male patient you'd been trying to save all morning. And you're crying.' He wiped her tears away with the pad of his thumb. 'So I'm guessing that set you worrying about your dad, and you just wanted to check he was OK.'

She swallowed. 'I was being wet.'

'No. You clearly love him very much. He's a lucky man.'

Did Lewis think her dad was lucky because she loved him? Or because her dad was loved?

And she knew that Lewis had lost his own father. 'Sorry. That wasn't tactful of me, considering...' She stopped. She had no idea if the grapevine knew about Lewis's father, and she didn't want to be the one to spill the story.

'It's OK.' He clearly guessed what she was thinking. 'Has that tea got sugar in it?'

She nodded. 'It's vile.'

'Good for shock.'

'Here.' She passed the mug to him.

He took a mouthful. 'You're right. It's vile. And it

doesn't make it better.' He sighed. 'Some days this job really sucks.'

'Today's one of those days,' she agreed.

He gave her a hug. 'Hang in there. I'll shout you a pizza after work. And you can choose all the toppings.'

'Oh, now that sounds interesting.' Eve, the charge nurse, came in to the staff kitchen. 'Date night, is it?'

'Not unless I was the last man on earth,' Lewis said lightly. 'Remember, Abby's already turned me down. Actually, Eve, you're just the person we need.'

'Me? Why?' Eve asked.

'Tough day.' He tipped his head to one side, indicating Abigail. 'Abby just lost a patient. Right now she needs hugs and carbs, but the carbs'll have to wait until after our shift ends. And your hugs are better than mine.' He patted Abigail's shoulder. 'I'll leave you in Eve's capable hands. But I'll shout you that pizza later. As I'd do for anyone in your shoes, and I'm sure you'd do it for me.'

'Thanks.'

Eve gave her a hug. 'It's always hard when you lose a patient.'

'The first one I've lost here.' Abigail grimaced. 'I'll never get used to this side of the job. I hate it.'

'You're only human, love.'

Abigail sighed. 'I guess I'd better get back to work. We have patients waiting.'

Eve patted her shoulder. 'Tomorrow will be a better day.'

Lewis was waiting for Abigail at the end of her shift.

'There's a nice pizzeria around the corner from me. We'll pick up a takeaway and I'll drive you home af-

terwards. What would you like me to order for you?'
he asked.

She shook her head. 'It's really sweet of you, but I
don't really think I want anything.'

'You have to eat something, Abby. Look, I'll order
for both of us.' He made a quick call. 'OK. It'll be ready
for us by the time we get there.'

Back at his flat, Abigail discovered that Lewis had
ordered a vegetarian special with artichokes, mush-
rooms and peppers. He also whipped up a quick rocket
and baby plum tomato salad and sprinkled shaved parmesan over the top.

She couldn't face eating but choked down a couple
of mouthfuls to be polite. After all, Lewis had made
the effort for her.

He looked at her and sighed. 'Oh, Abby.' He came
round to her side of the table, scooped her out of the
chair and settled her on his lap, then just held her, stroking her hair. 'Remember, we can't fix everyone. We do
the best we can and that's enough.'

'It isn't, though. Right now there's a family who's
missing their—' She stopped. Husband and father. Not
the most tactful thing to say. Lewis's family had been
in the same situation as Matthew's once. And, even
though it was a long time ago, she was pretty sure that
Lewis still missed his father.

'Maybe if he'd come to hospital sooner, we could've
helped him more. What was it?'

'His family doctor diagnosed him with flu. It turned
to sepsis.' She sighed. 'I had to send him up to ICU.'

'The sepsis was that bad?' He whistled. 'Abby, you
know as well as I do that once it gets to that stage there's
only a fifty-fifty chance of pulling through.'

'I know. But it still feels bad.'

'I don't know how to make you feel better.' He held her close. 'But I do think you shouldn't be alone tonight. Stay here with me. We'll get up early and I'll see you home in the morning.'

'I…'

'Stay,' he repeated softly. 'I can put your clothes through the washing machine and they'll be dry before morning.'

'Thank you.' She leaned against his shoulder. 'I'm sorry I'm being so wet. I don't often lose patients. And I'm afraid I don't deal with it very well.'

'Princess, nobody does. It's the downside of our job. Sometimes our patients are too ill for even the most experienced doctors to save them.'

'How do you deal with it when you lose a patient?' she asked.

'Go for a run. Push myself that bit harder, and do something physically demanding that I have to concentrate on so I don't have the time or the energy to think about what's happened.'

That was how he dealt with everything emotional, she thought. Except tonight. Tonight he was holding her.

'Come on. I'm not that hungry either. I'll run you a bath.'

Part of her wanted to protest that she was fine, that she could look after herself. But, just for once, it was good to let someone else take charge. To lean on someone and trust that they could support her.

'I don't have any girly bubble bath,' he warned. 'I do citrus and that's it. Nothing pink, nothing flowery.'

'Citrus is lovely,' she said.

And he'd left her a soft, fluffy bath robe next to the towels; she assumed it belonged to one of his sisters.

When she emerged from the bath, Lewis made her a mug of hot chocolate. Such a small thing, but it made her feel cherished.

Loved.

They curled up together on the sofa, watching re-runs of an old comedy series, with Lewis's arms wrapped tightly round her. He hadn't said the words but his actions tonight had told Abigail just how much he cared about her. The fact that he'd asked her to stay tonight, offered to share his space with her instead of driving her home—from Lewis that really meant something.

So maybe this relationship was more than just for fun. More than a fling.

Maybe it was time they opened up to each other.

Maybe it was time she told him the truth about herself.

Maybe tomorrow.

Finally she fell asleep, wrapped in his arms.

The next morning, Lewis woke up first. It felt odd, having someone asleep beside him. He'd made it a rule never to spend the night with a partner, not since Jenna.

But last night Abigail had been vulnerable. Upset. She'd needed him to comfort her.

He propped himself up on one elbow and watched her sleep. In repose, she was beautiful. She made him ache. And she scared him at the same time—because he wanted to do this again.

He really ought to back off a bit before both of them got hurt.

But then she woke up. Her smile was so sweet and so trusting it made his heart turn over.

'Thank you for last night, Lewis.' She cuddled into him. 'Sorry I was being so wet.'

'You weren't being wet. You'd had a rough day.' He just about stopped himself from saying, 'I'm glad I could be there for you.' Instead, he said, 'We're both on an early shift. Get dressed, and I'll drive you home.'

'There's no need, honestly.' She pressed a kiss against his shoulder. 'But you're right, I'd better get my skates on.'

'Your clothes are dry. I checked them last night. Feel free to use whatever you need in the bathroom.'

'Thank you. For everything,' she said softly.

And he had to really hold himself back from telling her that he wanted to give her more. That he wanted to wake up with her in the mornings and not have to rush back to his flat or for her to have to rush back to hers. That he wanted to move this thing between them on to the next step. That he wanted to try commitment.

He needed his head examined. Relationships didn't work for him. He couldn't have it all. He'd learned that the hard way.

So he just kissed her, smiled, and let her get dressed and walk out of the door.

Abigail didn't see Lewis that evening because she was seeing her dad, and their shifts clashed for the next couple of days, but they arranged to see each other on Saturday night.

'A quiet night in might be nice,' she said, inwardly planning nothing of the kind. 'There's a really good Chinese takeaway near me.'

'Sounds good,' Lewis said. 'Enjoy this evening with your dad.'

'I will.'

Was it her imagination or did he look slightly disappointed that she hadn't asked him to join them? Then again, she still hadn't told Lewis who her dad was.

And that could wait until Saturday.

Her father enveloped her in a warm hug as soon as she opened the door to him.

'Did you have a better day today?' he asked.

'Yes, and seeing you makes it even better.' Abigail hugged him.

He ruffled her hair. 'I love you. Let's go out and eat. I've found a really good place.'

'Where's your car?' she asked.

'Taxi tonight,' he said.

'All the way out to Surrey?'

'No, I'm staying over with Joe in Putney. And I don't want to drink and drive.' He gave her a hug. 'I'll take the lecture as read, darling.'

'Sorry. I know I'm dull. But I worry about you. And Joe, for that matter. He's practically my uncle.'

Keith smiled. 'I'll tell him that. He thinks a lot of you.'

Once the taxi had taken them to a plush restaurant in Mayfair and they'd settled at their table, Keith gave her a searching look. 'There's something different about you.'

'How do you mean?' she asked.

'For a start, you seem happier than you were at your last hospital.'

She nodded. 'The team's really nice. I've made friends.'

'Good.' He looked at her. 'And would one of those be a special friend?'

'No. I mean yes. I've met someone. But it's early days,' she said swiftly.

'And you don't want him to meet me yet.' He hid the hurt quickly, but Abigail had seen it in his expression. She reached over and squeezed his hand. 'I love you, Dad, and I'm so proud of you—but, no, I'm not ready for him to meet you yet. I don't think he'd be thrown by who you are, and I happen to know he likes your music, but...' How could she put this? 'He finds commitment hard,' she finished.

Keith sighed. 'You've fallen for a heartbreaker.'

'No. He's a good man. Honourable.'

'So you've fallen for him.'

She smiled. 'Dad, don't look so worried.'

'It's part of the job description—if you're a dad, you always worry about your daughter. Especially when it comes to this sort of thing.' He frowned. 'I might be pushing sixty now, but I can still pack a mean punch, even if he is about your age.'

She laughed. 'Don't go all alpha male on me. You're not going to need to punch him.'

'So are you going to tell me anything about him?'

'He's a doctor.'

'And?'

'He's a good man. You'd like him.' She rolled her eyes. 'He's an adrenalin fiend. I think he could be a bad influence on you. So let's make it clear right now—no swimming with sharks, no throwing yourself out of planes, and no ridiculous thrill rides at the amusement park, OK?'

Keith laughed. 'Isn't that meant to be my line?'

She laughed back. 'Actually, he's already done one of those with me. We went skydiving. And it was amazing. And, because you're over forty, you'd need a doctor's certificate before you'd be allowed in the plane, let alone anything else, so don't even think about it.'

'Noted, though I could point out that I'm not an old man yet.' He paused. 'As long as he's good to you. That's all I ask.'

'He's good to me.' She smiled. 'He was great yesterday, when I had my bad day.'

'Good. All right, I'll back off. For now,' Keith said.

He had her laughing with all sorts of scurrilous tales, and it was late when he finally saw her back to her flat.

'Thanks, Dad. I had a really good time tonight,' Abigail said.

'My pleasure.' He hugged her. 'You take care. And, um, let me know when you're ready for me to meet the man who swims with sharks and throws himself out of planes.'

'I will. And it'll be soon,' she promised. Because she was going to tell Lewis the truth about herself this weekend.

CHAPTER TEN

ON SATURDAY NIGHT, when they'd cleared away their plates and the cartons from the Chinese takeaway, Abigail brought out a brand-new pack of playing cards, still in the wrapper.

'What's this?' Lewis asked.

She tapped the cards. 'I seem to remember someone challenging me to a game of poker.'

He laughed. 'I think it was more like telling you never to play poker because your face is too expressive.'

'We'll see, shall we?'

'So what are the stakes?' he asked

She gave him a cheeky grin. 'I was thinking strip poker.'

'Are you quite sure about this, princess? Because I should warn you now that I had a misspent youth and I'm reasonably good at poker.'

'That's fine.' She smiled at him and handed him the playing cards. 'Shuffle and deal, Dr Gallagher.'

She lost the first three games. Deliberately. Two socks and her cardigan went onto the discard pile.

And then, just when Lewis was looking confident, she won five games straight. Enough to take him down to just his underpants.

'Well, well. And I thought you said you were reasonably good at this, Dr Gallagher,' she teased.

He narrowed his eyes at her. 'Why do I get the feeling that you just hustled me?'

She shrugged. 'It could be beginner's luck.' She stretched and leaned back against the sofa. 'Let's change the rules. Instead of losing a piece of clothing, we could answer a question instead.'

'Answer a question?'

She nodded. 'And we have to be totally honest with our answers.'

'Honest. Hmm. Are you quite sure you're not hustling me?'

In answer, she just smiled.

And she won the next game.

He blew out a breath. 'OK. Your question, princess.'

'I looked up how long it takes to qualify as a skydiving instructor,' she said. 'So how long exactly did you work for that training company?'

'I worked there part time before I took my A levels,' he said.

'That's too vague, Lewis. And we agreed honesty. How long?'

He sighed. 'Two years, while I was doing my A levels.'

'And then you took time out before university, didn't you?' she asked softly.

He closed his eyes. 'Yes.'

'Would I be right in thinking it was more than one gap year?'

'That's another question.'

She spread her hands. 'You and I both know I'll win the next game. Do you really want to drag it out?'

He opened his eyes and sighed. 'OK. I took six years out.'

'Six years?' She frowned. 'That's quite unusual. Why so many?'

'Where did you learn to play poker?' he countered.

'From a friend of my dad's. And you haven't finished answering the question.'

'Strictly speaking, it would be a new question and you haven't won a game.' His lips thinned. 'But you're a hustler. OK. Since you're asking. And I'm not going to insult you by asking that you keep this to yourself,' he said. 'It's something I don't talk about.' He looked at the floor.

'I told you my dad died when I was fourteen. My mum fell apart afterwards. It was as if she'd just frozen. She couldn't cope with anything. She just about managed to get up in the morning, but that was it. She sat in a chair all day long. She barely spoke to any of us. Obviously I knew later it was a mixture of grief and because she was reacting badly to anti-depressants—back then, family doctors used to hand them out without really thinking about whether it was the best option. But at the time I didn't have a clue what to do.'

Abigail stared at him, utterly shocked and unsure what to say. She'd had no idea.

'Then I overheard one of the neighbours saying we'd get taken into care and be split up if my mum wasn't careful.' He swallowed hard. 'I'd already lost my dad. I didn't want to lose my mum and my sisters, too. If we got taken away from her, no family would take the four of us on. Especially the ages we were. I knew we'd be split up and I might never see any of them again. So I thought that if I took over looking after us, we'd be able to stick together.'

Abigail couldn't quite take it in. 'You looked after your mum and your three sisters from when you were *fourteen*?'

'It was that or risk losing them,' he said simply. 'I wanted to keep my family together. And it was what Dad would've wanted me to do, too. Be the man of the house.'

'But you were only fourteen, Lewis. You were still a child.'

'I was old enough to learn how to cook and clean.' He shrugged. 'OK, so I burned a few things, and there was the time I didn't cook the chicken properly and we all had food poisoning the next day, but we managed.'

'That's pretty incredible. And I feel horrible now.' She blew out a breath. 'I accused you of learning to cook so you could score with girls.'

He spread his hands and gave her the fakest smile she'd ever seen in her life. 'Well, that worked pretty well for me at university.'

'I'm sorry.'

He shook his head. 'Don't pity me, Abby. It was my choice.'

'I'm not pitying you. But I'm sorry you had to grow up so early.' And sorry she'd pushed him into telling her all this. 'I see a very different man from the one the hospital grapevine sees.'

His face became set. 'Which is precisely why they don't know about it.'

'Now I know why you call your sisters your girls. You were pretty much a parent to them.'

He shrugged. 'Mum couldn't cope. There wasn't anyone else to step in. So that left me. And it was easy to get a part-time job at the training centre when I was sixteen, fitting it round my A levels—Dani was fourteen, by then, so she could take over some of the cooking and what have you. And that meant we had enough money to put food on the table and pay the bills.'

'How old's your youngest sister?' Abigail asked.

'Ronnie's the same age as you. Six years younger than me.'

She worked it out. 'So basically you stayed at home until the girls had all finished their A levels and left for university?'

'How could I walk away at eighteen and leave them to deal with Mum? They were still kids, Abby. Ronnie was only eight when Dad died. She was only halfway through primary school. She'd been at high school for a year when I finished my A levels. She needed stability. They all did. I couldn't just go and do whatever I wanted and leave them to sink.'

Abigail blew out a breath. 'Why didn't your mother get help?'

Lewis shrugged. 'I guess she was too proud.'

'Like your patient with alcoholic hepatitis,' she said, remembering. 'Too stressed and too proud to ask for help.'

'Or maybe she was too scared, in case the doctor called social services. She'd lost her husband. She needed to keep the rest of her family. If they'd seen how she was, that neighbour would've been right. Back then, the way social services were run, they would've taken us from her and put us into foster-care. Separately.'

'Why didn't any of your family or her friends do something to help?'

'She didn't give them the chance,' he said softly. 'She just closed off. Shut everyone out. Even the girls and me.' He wrinkled his nose. 'Anyway, it worked out OK. The girls all did well at school and went to university. And when Ronnie went to university, so did I.'

'You,' Abigail said, 'are a really good man.'

'I wish I was.' He shook his head. 'But I screwed up. Big time.'

She waited.

Eventually, he gave in and told her. 'A week after Ronnie and I went to university, my mum took an overdose. She couldn't cope with being on her own.'

'And you blame yourself for it? That's not fair, Lewis. It wasn't your fault.'

'I should've got her more support before I left, instead of just pulling the rug from under her. Or maybe I could've done it differently.'

It still shocked her that he blamed himself. 'You'd already put your own life on hold for six years, until your sisters had all finished school. It wouldn't be fair to expect you to put your life on hold forever.'

'Maybe. But I could've found a place to study nearer home, somewhere that I could commute, so I could keep an eye on Mum.'

She bit her lip. There wasn't a tactful way of asking this, but she needed to know. 'Did your mum…?'

He shook his head. 'They found her in time. And then she finally got the help she needed. Help I really should've made sure she got ten years before.'

'You were fourteen. You couldn't take responsibility for her crumbling, and you weren't to know what antidepressants do to people. If anything, that was your fam-

ily doctor's responsibility. They should've kept a better
eye on her instead of just writing out script after script.'

'It's how things were back then.' He sighed. 'I still
feel I should've done more for her.'

'You kept the family together from when you were
only fourteen years old, still a child yourself. You paid
the bills and you made sure everyone was fed, and you
deferred your own dreams of university for six years—
which is long enough for quite a few of them to have
refused to admission. There aren't many people who
would've done anywhere near that much, Lewis.'

He looked at her. 'You don't get it, do you?'

What more he could have done? No. But she understood something else now. No wonder he was an adrenalin fiend—he was making up now for the fun he'd
missed out on for most of his teens, when he'd taken
on responsibilities that had been way in advance of his
years. 'I get now why you don't want to get married and
settle down.' Because he'd already had the responsibility of bringing up a family.

'Good,' Lewis said.

She had a feeling there might be more to it than that,
but she'd already pushed him into telling her an awful
lot. Difficult stuff, too. Things he normally kept buried.
Right now, she thought, he needed a break.

She let him win the next game.

'You let me win,' he accused. And he looked annoyed about it.

'I wasn't patronising you.'

'No? It feels like it, princess.' This time, there was
an edge to his voice.

She shook her head. 'That wasn't my intention,
Lewis. Really.'

'I can't believe I told you never to play poker because you're easy to read.' He blew out a breath. 'You're a shark.'

'I played absolutely fairly,' she pointed out.

'And you normally play to win. The fact that you lost…'

She rolled her eyes. 'OK, so I threw the game. But it wasn't to patronise you. You've just told me a lot of really difficult stuff. I figured that you could do with some breathing space. So which item of clothing do you want me to remove?' She paused. 'Unless you want to remove it for me.'

'Nope. We're playing by your new rules now.' He looked her straight in the eye. 'So who exactly taught you poker, Abby?'

'I already told you that. One of my dad's colleagues.' On the tour bus. Keith had kept her clear of the crazy side of the rock 'n roll lifestyle, so going on tour for her had meant long, tedious hours spent with grownups who hadn't had much in common with her. But her dad's best friend and drummer had spent time with her while Keith had been writing, and he'd taught her how to play cards.

'That's not an exact answer, though, is it? Vague as anything. I want more than that, Abby. I want a *name*.'

She'd planned all along to tell him the truth about her background tonight, but now the time had come she felt sick with nerves. She wasn't ready yet. Maybe the name of her father's friend would pass him by. After all, Keith was the star of Brydon. Most people knew the name of the lead singer in a band and the lead guitarist, but the bass player and drummer tended to fade into the background. 'His name's Joe MacKenzie.'

Lewis's eyes narrowed. 'The same name as the drummer in Brydon.'

She squirmed. She should've guessed he'd know that. Lewis had a lot of music and he knew his stuff. 'It's a common enough name.'

'Not that common. And when you say he's your dad's colleague, I'm putting two and two together.'

'And coming up with more than four.'

'Am I?' He looked her straight in the eyes. 'Is your name really Smith?'

'Yes, it is. My turn to deal.'

He won. This time, not because she let him but because she couldn't concentrate.

'Right, Abby. What's your full name?'

Oh, help. This wasn't the way for him to find out. She had a feeling that he wasn't going to take it well.

But maybe she had to trust him. After all, he'd told her something important—something he was trusting her to keep to herself. She took a deep breath and threw his words back at him. 'OK. I'm not going to insult you by asking you to keep this to yourself. I know you won't rush to spill the beans to the hospital grapevine.'

'Uh-huh.'

'I was going to tell you anyway, but I hadn't worked out the right way to do it yet.' She lifted her chin. 'My full name's Cinnamon Abigail Brydon Smith.'

She saw the second the penny dropped. 'You're Keith Brydon's daughter. "Cinnamon Baby". That's you.'

'Yes. He wrote that song for me the day I was born. And the royalties over the years paid for this flat.' She dragged in a breath. 'That's why I go by my middle name. People are more likely to take me seriously. I mean, would you want to be treated by a doctor with a flaky name like Cinnamon?'

'Where does the Smith come from? Or is that your dad's real name?'

'It's my mum's.' She paused. 'She didn't marry my dad.' Or keep Abigail. Adeline Smith had left them both for a new love when Abigail had been four. So Keith had been forced to make a choice: give up his job to look after his daughter or take her on the road with him and employ a nanny-cum-governess. And Adeline hadn't been interested enough to see her daughter since.

His face was stony. 'You said your dad was a stockbroker.'

'No, *you* said he was a stockbroker. I just didn't correct you.'

'Abby, your dad's a famous rock star.'

'Yes, and I hate people seeing me as just the child of a famous person, not for who I am. I had years of it when I was small. Dad did his best to keep me out of the limelight, but the paparazzi loved the whole "Cinnamon Baby" story and they found ways of getting their shots.' She sighed. 'So I suppose you want to meet my dad now.'

He raised an eyebrow. 'Why do you say that?'

'Because my dad's Keith Brydon.'

'And?'

'Like you said. He's a rock star. Famous.'

'That doesn't have anything to do with you and me.'

'Doesn't it?'

Lewis frowned. 'Is that why you don't date? Because you think once people find out who you are, they'll stop being interested in you and want to hang out with your dad?'

'It happens.' Her voice was expressionless.

'I like your dad's music, yes, and it might be nice to meet him some time. But that'll be because he's *your* dad, not because he's Keith Brydon.'

Exactly what she'd told her father. But right now she was having a tough time believing it. Believing that Lewis really was different from the people she'd thought were her friends or partners in the past.

'Abby…' He leaned forward and kissed her lightly on the mouth. 'You really have had lousy taste in men.'

'Not just men. It was all the way through.'

Now she'd started talking, her tongue was running away with her. This wasn't supposed to happen. She tried to stop it, but Lewis was a trained doctor, too, and he knew the same waiting trick that she did. And the words just kept spilling out.

'My mum left us for someone else when I was four.'

Lewis frowned. 'Why didn't she take you with her?'

Abigail sighed. 'Dad would never say. But I think it's because I would've cramped her style and the other guy didn't want a brat hanging round.' She shrugged. 'At least Dad wanted me. He got custody of me officially and kept me with him. I was home-schooled until I was fourteen, and I used to travel with him when he was on tour. Then he realised that it wasn't much fun for me— you wouldn't believe how tedious it is, being on a tour bus. Day after day after day, moving from one town to another, never getting time to actually see anything of whatever country you're touring in because you have a rigid schedule, so all you see is the inside of the bus and the inside of the hotel.

'That's why Joe taught me to play cards. I ran out of books on one tour and he noticed how bored I was.'

She grimaced. 'And Dad knew I wanted to be a doctor when I grew up. So he said after that he'd just tour in the school holidays so I could go to a proper school and do my exams, and we settled in Surrey.'

'But?' Lewis asked softly.

'But I never fitted in at school.' She shrugged. 'I'd spent all my life hanging around adults so I wasn't used to being around kids, and I didn't have a clue how to make friends. I wasn't used to the way the pack works. How to be popular, how to make people like me. And I'd spent all my time with guys—the band, the roadies. Even my tutor was male. I didn't know how to connect with girls, be part of a group.'

She stared at the floor. 'Sometimes I wonder if things would've been different if my mum had stuck around. If she would've taught me how to do the girly stuff.' She looked at Lewis. 'But even if she'd taken me with her, I don't think she would've loved me as much as Dad does.'

'Do you miss her?'

Abigail shook her head. 'I don't really remember much about her. I suppose you can't really miss what you've never had. Yes, sometimes I wish I had a mum to talk to. There are some things I'd rather not discuss with Dad.' She shrugged again. 'I'm just not good with other people. And I got a fair bit of hassle at school because of my name. You wouldn't believe how many stupid little names they made up for me. Every spice they could think of, every nickname for someone with red hair, every word that started with "sin". On and on and on. It was relentless.

'One of the teachers found me crying after school one day, and she suggested to Dad that maybe I should use my middle name instead. Because it was a bit more—well, normal.'

'But it wasn't enough to stop the other kids teasing you?'

She swallowed miserably. 'I thought I was starting to make friends after that. Then I overheard some of them talking. They said the only reason they were hanging around with me was because they hoped I'd invite them to a party at my place, and they'd meet all these pop stars. Which is ironic, because Dad didn't hang out with the kind of bands they liked. They wouldn't have recognised any of the musicians he knew.' She gave a mirthless laugh. 'I really wasn't happy at that school. Dad moved me to a different school, and from then on I was known as Abigail Smith. It was better after that.'

'I'm glad.'

And, damn him, he waited. As if he knew that there was more. The words bubbled to the surface. 'But the guy I met when I was seventeen…I really thought he loved me. It turned out he was only interested because he knew who my dad was, and hoped Dad would get him a recording contract.'

'And you found that out the same way as the girls at school, because you overheard him talking to someone?'

'No.' She bit her lip. 'We had a fight when I said I wouldn't sleep with him until I was eighteen. He called me a stupid kid and lost his temper. That's when he told me he wasn't interested in me anyway—he'd only been with me because he wanted to get close to my dad. I had no idea he'd even known who my dad was—especially as everyone knew me as Abigail Smith by then, rather than Cinnamon Brydon. I guess I must've confided in someone at some point, and it leaked out. That, or someone had seen us together and worked it out.'

Lewis stroked her hair. 'Not everyone's out for what they can get.'

'I know. But university wasn't much better. It was the same thing—I never really fit in. I was always on the outside, and the only time I was ever invited in was when they found out who I was. Every man I dated…as soon as they found out who Dad was, things changed. And not for the better. I guess that's when I started keeping myself separate so I didn't get hurt anymore.'

'It doesn't have to be like that.' He paused. 'Newsflash for you, princess. People in the emergency department at the London Victoria like you for who you are. Now you've started opening up and letting people close, you've given them the chance to like you. And they do like you, Abby.'

'Sydney and Marina—they've been kind.'

'It's called being your friend.' He paused. 'But you're scared it'll change if they find out who you are.'

'It always does,' she said bleakly.

'Is that why you left your last hospital?'

'No. I wanted the special reg job, so I applied to the London Victoria. That's why I moved.'

'And you work in emergency medicine because of your dad.'

She nodded. 'It's like you said—a couple of rounds of golf in the week doesn't make up for a sedentary lifestyle. Sure, when Dad's touring, he's active—but when he's writing music or just practising at home, he doesn't do any real exercise, not much more than a couple of rounds of golf in the week. He eats the wrong stuff and he doesn't eat regular meals—sometimes he even forgets to eat. His hours are nothing like a normal person's hours, and he drinks way too much. He doesn't do drugs, so I guess that's one thing I don't have to worry about—but I do worry about him having a heart attack or a stroke or ending up with a fatty liver.'

She blew out a breath. 'I guess if I can keep saving someone's dad in Resus, I feel that what goes around comes around. And if my dad ever ends up in Resus then someone will save him. I know it's stupid and superstitious, but I can't help it.'

'That's why you rang him when you lost your patient.'

'Yes. I just needed to be sure that he was OK.' She sighed. 'I wish he'd find someone who makes him happy. Someone who'll love him and look after him and do all the wifely nagging stuff to make him eat properly and do a bit of gentle exercise.'

'Why hasn't he found someone else? Is he still in love with your mum?'

'I don't think so. But it probably didn't help, being a single dad—I remember him having a couple of girlfriends when I was younger, but he overheard one being rude to me about the colour of my hair. I never saw her again after that day, so I guess he dumped her.'

'Good for him. You should always put your kids first.'

Something, she thought, that his own mother hadn't done for him. Lewis's mother had opted out, leaving him to pick up the pieces and look after his sisters.

It must've shown in her expression because he said, 'Don't judge my mother.'

She flushed. 'Lewis, she let you deal with everything when you were still a child.'

'She really loved my dad. He was her whole world. Losing him totally devastated her. And not everyone's strong enough to cope with something like that.' He looked grim. 'She's never been involved with anyone since because she says nobody can ever match up to him. I can understand why she crumbled. The loss was just too great.'

'But she's OK now?'

He nodded. 'She went through the mill a bit, coming off the anti-depressants. She'd been on them for way too long. And at the moment things aren't great between us. She feels so guilty about not being there for us when we were kids and for dumping her responsibilities on me. I've told her it doesn't matter, but she just can't get past the guilt—and she shuts us all out.

'Manda was hoping that Louise being born would help break the ice a bit, but it hasn't. Mum doesn't trust herself not to let us all down again so she's pretty much a hands-off grandma. It's pretty awkward when we do see each other. So right now I email her once a week, just to say hello and see how she is. Just keeping the lines of communication open.' He grimaced. 'It's better than calling her. At least in an email there aren't any long, difficult silences. You can sound bright and breezy—you know, smile from the wrists up.'

'That's hard for you.'

He waved a dismissive hand. 'I cope.'

By doing all the adrenalin-fiend stuff. It meant he didn't have time to think or feel. Now she was really beginning to understand him.

He looked at her. 'I never would've thought you were the child of a wild rock star. Didn't you ever want to be a singer or play guitar?'

'No. I probably take after my mother—not that I know for definite, as we're not in touch. I did try to get in contact with her when I was eighteen but she wasn't interested: she had a new life.' Somewhere else she didn't fit in. 'I suppose, seeing all the rock-star lifestyle, I just went the other way,' she said dryly.

'I didn't join in and do the parties and the late nights and the smashing up of hotel rooms. I guess it's like someone who runs away from the circus to be a book-keeper—swapping all the chaos for something secure. And it was chaos, when it wasn't endless travelling. I love my dad, but I really can't live the way he does.' She blew out a breath. 'This wasn't how tonight was meant to go.'

'Baring souls, you mean?'

'I was just hoping you'd open up to me a little bit. Let me understand you a bit more.'

'But you didn't bargain on that lot,' he said wryly.

'No. And I didn't mean to dump all that lot on you either.'

He raked a hand through his hair. 'I feel pretty wiped.'

'So do I,' she admitted. 'Lewis—let's just go to bed.'

His eyes widened. 'You want sex *now*?'

'No.' She looked at him, shocked. 'I just want to hold you. And for you to hold me. Like you did the other night. Maybe we can give each other some comfort. Maybe everything will look a bit better in the morning.'

'Maybe.'

Except it wasn't. Eventually Abigail fell asleep, but Lewis couldn't. Every time he began to drift off, he woke up with a start, panic seeping through his veins.

He felt as if he were stuck to the bed, pinned down by a cold, heavy weight.

Responsibility.

Commitment.

This was a mess. Part of him wanted to stay; part of him wanted to run. And he knew what the problem was. What was making him panic so much.

He was in love with Abigail Smith.

Given his track record, it was all going to go wrong. Both of them would end up hurt.

He already knew that Abigail had been hurt in the past. The feeling of never fitting in. The feeling of people only seeing her as Keith Brydon's daughter, not for herself. The people in her past who'd used her to further their own careers and social ambitions, not caring that they were trampling on her.

She deserved better.

A lot better.

And she needed someone who could commit to her. Someone who'd put her first in his life, someone who'd love her and cherish her.

Much as Lewis wanted it to be him, he knew he couldn't do it. He just couldn't handle commitment.

So there was only one thing he could do. The right thing. Even though it was going to hurt like hell, it was much better to do it now than to let it drag on and hurt them both even more.

Quietly, carefully he wriggled out of bed. Abigail stirred and Lewis froze, willing her to go back to sleep. Her breathing became even again and he grabbed his clothes. It took only a few moments to put them all on once he'd left the bedroom.

Part of him knew that he ought to leave a note, but

he didn't have a clue what to say, and he didn't want to wait around while he thought about it in case she woke.

Hating himself for being so unfair to her but not knowing what else to do, he let himself quietly out of her flat and headed for home.

CHAPTER ELEVEN

ABIGAIL'S ALARM SHRILLED; she groped for the clock on her bedside table, hit the snooze button and rolled over towards Lewis.

Except his side of the bed was empty.

And, given that the sheet was cold, it had obviously been empty for quite some time. Maybe he hadn't been able to sleep and had got up to make himself a coffee without disturbing her; maybe he was reading a journal on the sofa while he waited for her to wake up.

But when she padded into the kitchen, it was empty and the kettle was cold. The living room was equally empty.

Which meant he'd left.

Without even leaving a note.

So much for thinking that everything would be better this morning. What an idiot she was. She'd pushed him way too far last night. She was pretty sure he was going to break up with her now; the worst thing was, there was absolutely nothing she could do about it.

She wished she hadn't made him talk to her, wished she hadn't spilled out her own insecurities. Of course he wasn't going to want to know her now. How could she have been such a fool?

She was glad she was on duty that morning and he wasn't. It would give them both a bit of space and would mean that she didn't have time to brood about the way he'd left without even saying goodbye. She was as bad as he was, she thought wryly, using work in the same way that he used his adrenalin-fiend stuff. But it helped.

All the same, she was disappointed not to find a text from him or anything when she left the hospital and checked her phone. Maybe he was doing family stuff with his sisters. A chill ran through her. Or maybe he was just working out the right way to end it with her.

Lewis couldn't settle to anything. Not while this whole thing of letting Abigail down gently was hanging over him. He was off duty, and he knew that Abigail was working. He thought about texting her, but he knew that this was something he had to do face to face: it was the only fair way. He wasn't going to be a coward about it, even though he didn't like what he was about to do.

How did you break up with someone?

It had always been easy enough for him in the past. But the difference was those women hadn't mattered. Abigail did.

'It's not you. It's me.'

That was true enough. But it sounded weak. As if he was making excuses.

He brooded about it all day. He went for a run in the late afternoon, but the exercise didn't clear his head and make him feel better, the way it usually did.

He had to see her. Chances were she'd go straight home from her shift. Though he'd left it too late to buy her flowers or anything; the only places left open would be corner shops and garage forecourts, and they'd hardly have something special. He shook himself. Flowers probably weren't appropriate anyway. Goodbye, and here's a bunch of roses? Hardly.

No. He needed to do this like you'd take off a sticking plaster—firm, fast and final.

Lewis ended up driving over to Abigail's flat. He called her on his mobile phone when he'd parked the car.

'Lewis?'

He really hated himself for the sound of the hope in her voice. Hope that he was about to stamp over in hobnailed boots. 'We need to talk. Can I come and see you?' he asked.

'When?'

'Now. I'm outside,' he explained.

'Oh.' She sounded wary now. 'You'd better come up, then.'

He practised the words all the way up to her flat, under his breath.

Abigail answered the door, looking tired and unhappy, and he felt even guiltier. 'Do you want a coffee?' she asked.

'No, thanks.'

She closed the door behind him and ushered him into the living room, but he didn't sit down.

'You didn't leave a note,' she said.

He could see the hurt in her face, and hated himself for it. 'Sorry.' He shook his head. 'I didn't know what to write.'

'Uh-huh. So what did you want to talk about?' she asked.

He took a deep breath. 'I've been thinking. You and I—we want different things out of life. It's really not going to work between us, so I think the best thing we can do is to go back to being just colleagues.'

She said nothing.

He raked a hand through his hair. 'Abby, it was always going to be nothing more than a fling between us. I told you right from the start that I don't want to get married and settle down to have kids. I never promised you a happy ending.'

'I guess I should be grateful that I lasted more than three dates.'

That hurt—she knew he was more than the image he projected at the hospital—but he guessed he deserved it. Because he knew he'd just hurt her, really badly. 'I'm sorry. I hope you find—'

'Don't,' she cut in. 'Just don't. OK. You've said what you want to say. End of story. Please, just go.'

'Abby—'

'No.' Without saying another word, she marched to the front door, opened it and waited for him to leave.

He walked through the door, knowing there was no way back, and feeling like the meanest bastard under the sun.

But he'd done the right thing.

He *had*.

Abigail closed the door and sank down to the floor, her back sliding against the wall. She wrapped her arms round her legs and rested her chin on her knees.

She'd guessed this was coming. But she hadn't expected it to hurt so much.

It was her own fault. How stupid she'd been to hustle Lewis at cards, to push him into talking before he was really ready for it. And then she'd dumped all her own insecurities onto him. No wonder he'd run a mile. It had all been too much, too soon.

And now it was over.

So much for thinking that they had something special. That they could move their relationship on to the next step. The whole thing had just blown up in her face.

And there was nobody she could talk to about it. How ironic that he'd asked her if she missed her mother. Right then Abigail could really do with a mother figure to talk to, to help her make sense of all this mess. But there was nobody. If she confided in her friends at work, it would make things awkward in the department. She didn't want her dad to worry about her. The only other person she could maybe talk to was Joe, but then she knew he'd tell her dad, so that was a no-no as well.

Which left…

Nobody.

Well, she'd just have to deal with it on her own. She was used to being on her own. What was the difference now?

Abigail slept badly, and ended up using way too much concealer to disguise the dark shadows under her eyes before she went to work the next morning. Luckily she and Lewis were rostered in different sections of the department so she didn't actually have to work with him, and it was easy enough to give an anodyne smile when she had to. Everyone knew she was quiet and shy so they didn't expect much from her; for once, she was really grateful for her ice princess reputation.

She concentrated on her patients during her shifts at the hospital and tried to drown out her memories after work by studying hard. Give it enough time, and the physical ache of missing Lewis would go.

It had to.

Seeing Abigail at work was hard. She was quiet, barely smiled, and she'd gone right back into her shell—and Lewis knew that it was all his fault.

What he hadn't expected was how miserable he felt without Abigail. How much he missed her quiet common sense, her shy smile, that sweet, wide-eyed look when he'd kissed her until she'd been dizzy.

Had he just made the biggest mistake of his life?

He knew he could trust her. Abigail hadn't said a thing about his family or his background to anyone. No way would the hospital grapevine pass up such juicy material.

And she wasn't like Jenna. She'd never made any demands on him. She didn't expect him to choose between her and his family, and she never would—that wasn't Abigail's style.

He tried to talk to her a couple of times, but she pretty much blanked him. Which he knew he deserved.

He was going to have to do something really spectacular to get her to talk to him. He needed to think about it, but for now he wasn't going to make a fuss at the hospital. The last thing either of them needed was to be the topic of gossip. But somehow he was going to persuade her to talk to him. And maybe, just maybe, she might forgive him for being an idiot and give him another chance.

On Wednesday, Abigail ducked out of lunch with Marina and Sydney, claiming that she was caught up with a patient.

But at the end of what should've been her lunch break they found her in the office where she was doing paperwork and closed the door behind them.

She looked up at them and forced a smile. 'Sorry I didn't make lunch.'

'But you had a patient you couldn't leave,' Sydney said.

'And then all the paperwork,' Abigail confirmed. 'You know what it's like.'

'I've used enough avoidance tactics in my time to know when other people are using them, Abby,' Marina said gently. 'Have you even had a sandwich at your desk?'

'I…' She couldn't lie. 'No,' she said dully. She hadn't felt much like eating.

'I thought not. So we brought you these from the cafeteria.' Marina handed her a latte and a raspberry muffin.

'Not just the sweet stuff. And we remembered that you're vegetarian.' Sydney placed a brie and tomato baguette in front of her.

'I…' There was a lump in Abigail's throat. 'That's really kind of you.'

'No, it's not kind. It's because you're our friend and we can tell you're upset about something. We're worried about you,' Sydney said.

The lump in Abigail's throat got even bigger.

'What's happened, Abby?' Marina asked.

She sighed. She wasn't going to get away with this, was she? But maybe they'd be satisfied with the barest of details. 'I was seeing someone. We, um, split up on the weekend.'

'He's an idiot,' Sydney said immediately. 'Why would he break up with someone as lovely as you?'

Abigail wasn't going to break Lewis's confidences by explaining. 'It just didn't work out.'

'And you were in love with him?'

'Yes.' She bit her lip. 'Sorry, I'd rather not talk about it.' And she really didn't want them to guess who she'd been seeing. Thank God she and Lewis had kept their relationship quiet or the hospital grapevine would be unbearable.

'Girly night out required, I think,' Marina said. 'To-night we'll go and see a really girly rom-com and then eat our combined body weight in ice cream. And no excuses, Abby. You need to go out and do something to take your mind off him. And just remember the guy's an idiot.'

'How do you know it's not my fault?'

'Because you're nice. You're not high-maintenance or difficult,' Sydney said with a smile, and patted her shoulder. 'Let's meet outside Leicester Square station at half past six.'

The film was good, but Abigail found it hard to concentrate. She kept thinking of the night when Lewis had brought ice cream over to her flat and suffered the second half of a film he'd loathed, just so he could hold her.

It wasn't going to happen again.

And in future she wasn't going to make the mistake of losing her heart to anyone. Lewis had it right. Three dates and you're out. That was the way to protect yourself.

Working in the same department for the next week was almost unbearable. They'd gone back to the formal Dr

Smith and Dr Gallagher. It was worse even than when Abigail had first met Lewis and had thought him charming and as shallow as a puddle. Because now she knew the real man—and he was so far from what the hospital grapevine said about him it was untrue.

Several times he tried to talk to her, but she couldn't just pretend they were friends—not just yet. It was still too raw. She needed some distance. Changing her job was out of the question, her promotion was far too recent. So she'd just have to grit her teeth and get on with it.

At the end of the week Abigail was rostered in Resus with Lewis. She'd known that she'd have to face this situation at some point, and she managed to cope just fine, being cool and professional and acting as if they barely knew each other.

Until the last patient on their shift.

Biddy, the paramedic, did the handover. 'This is Jack. He's fifty-eight and was complaining of chest pains. He said it felt like an elephant was sitting on his chest.'

Abigail went cold. She knew that was a classic symptom of a heart attack.

'We gave him GTN spray under his tongue, but it didn't have any effect.'

Abigail went colder still. If the pain didn't ease with glyceryl trinitrate, that was a bad sign.

'And the trace we ran off shows signs of an MI.'

Myocardial infarction. The thing Abigail worried about more than anything else with her dad—and this man was exactly the same age as her dad.

'We've given him oxygen and aspirin, and cannulated him,' Biddy finished.

'Thank you,' Abigail said quietly.

'Have you given him an anti-emetic yet?' Lewis asked

'No,' Biddy said.

'OK. I'm on it. Thanks, Biddy.' Lewis administered the anti-emetic swiftly and had the leads of an ECG in place so they could monitor the activity in Jack's heart.

Abigail was about to give Jack some more drugs when the monitor changed.

'He's in VT,' Lewis said.

Ventricular tachycardia was where the lower chamber of the heart beat too fast; the abnormal rhythm of the heart could be life-threatening.

'Crash team, ready. Can you take the upper layers of Jack's clothing off, ready for the paddles?' she asked. She knew that really Lewis ought to be leading, as he was her senior colleague, but this case was important to her. She needed to feel that she was the one making the difference. He caught her eye, and she knew from his expression that he understood how she felt and would let her carry on.

She put the paddles in place. 'Charging to two hundred and clear,' she said.

Everyone stood back with their hands off the patient.

'Shocking now,' she said.

'Still in VT,' Lewis reported.

'Charging to two hundred again,' she said, 'and clear. Shocking now.'

Still there was no response.

Come on, come on, she willed Jack. You have to get through this. Keep the karma going, so if the worst happens to Dad someone will be able to save him.

'Charging to three-sixty. And clear,' she said.

Thank God, the monitor showed the rhythm she was looking for: normal sinus waves. It was going to be all right.

'No pulse,' Lewis said.

No. No. *No*. This couldn't be happening. It meant Jack's heart wasn't pumping blood round his body, and she knew the odds were rapidly stacking up against them.

Life support algorhythm. Now. 'Can you bag while I do the compressions?' she asked Lewis.

'Are you sure you don't want me to do the compressions?'

'I'm sure.'

She administered the drugs she hoped would make Jack's heart respond and went through the basic sequence of life support. Ten repetitions, checking for a pulse between each one.

No pulse.

No change on the monitor.

Please, please, respond, she begged inwardly.

'Giving more epinephrine,' she said, and continued with the chest compressions, fifteen to two of Lewis's bagged breaths.

Still nothing

'We'll keep going,' she said.

Dawn, the triage nurse, came in. 'His family's here.'

Abigail shook her head. 'I don't want them to see this. It's not fair on them. Can you take them off to a side room, please?'

'Sure.'

After another twenty minutes, Lewis placed his hand on her wrist. 'He's been without oxygen too long now, Abby. He's gone.'

'No.'

'We need to call it.'

'No.' She knew he was right, but she couldn't do it. Fear flared up inside her, making her cold.

'Abby, if I have to pull rank, I will. Call it,' he said grimly.

She closed her eyes. 'Everyone agreed?' she whispered.

One by one, everyone agreed.

She looked at the clock. 'Time of death, sixteen thirty-four.'

'Do you want me to talk to the family?' he asked.

'No. I'll do it.' She couldn't face the concern on his face either, and walked out of the room before he said something that cracked her composure completely.

Jack's wife and daughter were waiting in the office where Dawn had put them. They looked up hopefully as Abigail opened the door.

'I'm so sorry,' she said, and their faces crumpled.

Jack's daughter looked to be about her own age. Heavily pregnant, too, so he hadn't even had the chance to meet his grandchild. It felt as if someone had reached into Abigail's chest and was squeezing her heart.

If it had been her own father, there would only be one person in the room, waiting to hear the news. Her. And that thought was unbearable.

She sat with Jack's family for a while, answering their questions and being as kind as she could. Then she went back into the office, on autopilot. It was near the end of the working day, but there was just enough time for her to call the coroner and get in touch with Jack's GP.

She put the phone down and leaned back in the chair,

closing her eyes. Today was definitely the worst day she'd spent at the London Victoria.

'OK, princess?' a voice asked softly.

Oh, no.

Lewis.

She kept her eyes closed. 'What are you doing here?'

'Checking up on you.'

'I'm fine,' she lied.

'Abby. I was there the last time you lost a patient.'

He'd cradled her and cherished her, made her feel loved—and, only a few days later, he'd dumped her. She gulped down the sob that threatened to escape. 'And?' she drawled, aiming to sound completely unbothered by his presence.

'And I know why this case is going to upset you even more. Jack was the same age as your dad.'

Trust him to go right to the heart of it. Tortured, she opened her eyes and looked at him. 'And I didn't save him.'

'Neither did I. Nor did anyone else on the team. You know the odds, Abby. Nobody could've done more. Nobody could've saved him.'

And then he did the one thing that made her crack.

He stood there in front of her with his arms open. All she had to do was stand up, walk into them and he'd hold her close. Make her feel warm again. Make the bad feelings go away.

Right now she was just too miserable and it was way, way too tempting. She stood up and walked into his arms.

He cradled her, just as he had the night she'd lost Matthew, resting his cheek against her hair and stroking her back.

But this was all wrong. They weren't together any more. And it hurt too much for her to stay here in his arms.

She pulled away. 'I can't do this. Leave me alone, Lewis.'

'Abby, it doesn't have to be like this,' he began.

'Yes, it does.'

'Abby.' He took a step towards her.

She couldn't handle this. And the only thing she could think of to do was to rush out of the office to the nearest toilet and lock herself in. Unless Lewis was going to make a scene—and, given how much he hated the hospital grapevine, she was pretty sure that wasn't going to happen—he'd have to give up and leave her alone.

Lewis stared at the locked door in exasperation.

OK. She'd won this round.

But she was going to have to go home tonight, and he had every intention of being there on her doorstep. And he'd wait for as long as it took.

CHAPTER TWELVE

ABIGAIL WALKED HOME from the hospital with a heavy heart. Her legs felt like lead and it was a real effort to put one foot in front of the other. Her dad was in the studio, so his mobile phone was switched to voicemail; not wanting him to worry, she hadn't left him a message. Maybe she could ring Sydney or Marina—they'd been there for her earlier in the week. But if she spoke to them she'd have to explain about Lewis, and then it would get complicated in the department.

Which left nobody to talk to about the situation.

Right then, Abigail felt more isolated and alone than she'd ever felt in her entire life.

Where had she gone so wrong?

When she reached the corner of her road, she saw someone sitting on the step at the entrance to her block. She frowned. Why would anyone be waiting there? Had someone forgotten their key? As she drew nearer, she realised it was Lewis.

Oh, no. She really wasn't in the mood for a confrontation. And she'd made it pretty clear at the hospital that she wanted him to leave her alone. Why was he sitting there, waiting for her?

Gritting her teeth, she walked up to him. 'What do you want?'

'To talk to you.'

'I don't think there's anything to say.'

'I do.'

She shook her head. 'Leave me be, Lewis.'

'Abigail, please. Just give me five minutes. When I've said what I've got to say, if you still want me to go, I promise I'll go.'

'I'll give you two minutes,' she said. And that was more than he deserved.

'Two minutes,' he agreed.

She let him into the block and he followed her up the stairs to her first-floor flat in silence. Taking a deep breath, she opened her front door and let him in.

She knew the courteous thing would be to offer him a drink, but right at that moment she wasn't feeling particularly polite. 'So what do you want, Lewis?' She knew it sounded grumpy and ungracious, but she didn't care.

'To apologise, for starters—and to explain.' He sighed. 'I don't know where to start. I could've brought you half a florist's to say sorry. I could've hired a sky-writer and had it written in huge letters in the sky. Or I could've sent you up in a plane and written you a message on the beach that was big enough for you to read from the plane. But, with your background, big showy gestures like that…'

The type he'd normally rely on, she thought.

He shrugged. 'Well, they don't really mean anything.'

'They don't,' she said. 'They're just an ego-boost for the person making the gesture, or something a publicist has dreamt up. There's no real heart in it.'

'Exactly. So what you're getting is me. No flowers, no fancy trappings—just me, talking from the heart.'

She gave a mirthless laugh. 'You're over-egging it, Lewis.'

'Probably,' he agreed with a grimace. 'I don't mean to. I'm not good at this sort of thing. So I'll cut to the chase. I'm sorry I hurt you, Abby.'

She shrugged. 'I'm a big girl. I'll get over it.'

'I was wrong. I've been an idiot.' He shook his head in apparent frustration. 'I've thrown away something very special, just because I was scared.'

This was the man who threw himself off zip-lining platforms and out of planes and thought nothing of it. He didn't have a fearful bone in his body. 'There's actually something an adrenalin fiend is scared of?' she asked, her tone a shade more caustic than she intended.

'Yes. Lots of things.' He paused. 'Bottom line—because I realise I'm running out of time here—will you give me another chance?'

She looked at him. 'Do you have any idea how miserable I've been this week?'

'If it's anything like the way I've been feeling, yes. And I'm sorry. I wish I could take it all back.'

'You can't change the past.'

'But you can learn from it—and I realise now that I've spent half my life being wrong. Keeping people at a distance.' He held her gaze. 'Just like you do.'

She narrowed her eyes at him. 'I don't treat people the way you do. Three dates and you're out.'

'You don't even give them one,' he pointed out. 'You don't let them close.'

'And you do all the adrenalin-fiend stuff so you don't have to face anything emotional,' she countered.

'Running away from my feelings? Yes, you're right.

I do. It's easier.' He paused. 'Just so you know, it scared the hell out of me when I asked you to stay with me that night. I never let anyone stay with me, and I never stay overnight with anyone. When I woke up in the morning next to you, I knew I wanted to do it again. And that scared me even more.'

She frowned. 'Why didn't you tell me? I thought you couldn't wait to get rid of me.'

'Because I was scared it was all going to go wrong.' He spread his hands. 'OK, fine. I've used up my two minutes. I'll get out of your hair.'

She could let him walk away.

Or she could let him talk. Tell her why he was so scared of commitment.

And maybe—just maybe—they could find a way forward through this.

'You said,' she reminded him, 'that it was my decision whether or not to kick you out after you'd had your two minutes' say.'

He winced. 'I didn't put it quite like that but, yes. If you want me to go, I'll go.'

She needed to be clear about where this was heading. 'You really want me to give you another chance? You want me back?'

'Yes.'

'You're quite sure about that?'

He looked her straight in the eye. 'More sure than I've been about anything in my entire life.'

'Then I need to understand why you dumped me.'

He winced. 'Because I thought it would be better to end it now than let us get even closer and have it all go wrong—when it would hurt us both more.'

She frowned. 'Why did you think it would go wrong in the first place?'

* * *

She really wasn't going to make it easy for him, was she? Then again, he didn't deserve an easy ride. He'd hurt her.

'I guess I owe you an explanation.' But telling her... The words stuck in his throat. 'I've never told anyone this before. Not even the girls.' Especially not them. He hadn't wanted his sisters to think that he'd sacrificed his happiness and his future for them. Piling on the guilt like that wasn't fair.

'I'm listening,' Abigail said.

'I met Jenna when I was twenty-three. She was a client at the training centre. She gave me her number at the end of her course and asked me to call her.' He blew out a breath. 'We started dating. I fell head over heels in love with her. And I asked her to marry me. I even bought her a ring. It wasn't an expensive one—I was supporting Mum and the girls, so I didn't exactly have much spare cash—but I always planned to buy her a better one later, when I could afford it.'

And then it had all gone wrong. 'She asked me to move in with her.' He looked away. 'I told her I couldn't even think about it until the girls were settled. OK, so Dani was doing her finals and Manda was in her first year at university, but Ronnie was still only seventeen, and I was applying to university to read medicine. I asked Jenna to wait for me.' He dragged in a breath. 'She wasn't happy about it. I guess she wanted me to stay, put her before my family and my dreams of being a doctor.'

Abigail frowned. 'If she'd really loved you, she would've understood the situation and waited. You weren't exactly old. You had plenty of time.'

'That was my thinking. But she didn't want to wait four years for me to finish university and then another two more years for me to qualify.' He knew he was going to have to tell Abigail the rest of it. The bit he never talked about.

'Then she told me she was pregnant. She was on the pill, but she claimed she'd forgotten to take it.' He grimaced. 'And I was horrible. I thought she'd done it on purpose. I felt trapped—just when I thought my life was going to start, it was all over and I was saddled with responsibilities again.' He blew out a breath. 'But of course I was going to stand by her. I wouldn't abandon her.'

'So you got married and had the baby?' Abigail asked.

He shook his head. 'It turned out that she wasn't pregnant at all. She'd just said that because she knew I'd do the right thing by her, and it was the only way she could think of to stop me leaving my job and going to university.' He rubbed a hand across his face. 'I only know because she fell out with her best friend over it—and her best friend thought I deserved to know the truth.'

'What did you do?'

'Asked her straight out.' He sighed. 'She admitted it. And I broke it off with her. I couldn't be with someone who'd lie to me over something that big. I know you should put your partner first, but she wasn't prepared to see that I had needs, too. She wasn't prepared to compromise.' He sighed. 'I learned the hard way that you couldn't have it all.'

'I'm not Jenna,' Abigail said.

'I know that.'

'I'd never ask you to choose between me and your family or your dreams. Just as I know you wouldn't ask me to choose between you and my dad.'

'Of course I wouldn't.'

'And I'd never lie about being pregnant. That isn't fair on anyone.'

'I know.'

'But that's why you don't do commitment?'

'Yes. Because, in my experience, it's going to blow up in my face. And you have issues, too,' he pointed out. 'You worry about not fitting in.'

'That's because I *don't* fit in.'

'Maybe that was true in your last hospital, and at schools that—well, you were home-schooled for so long. Of course school wasn't going to work for you. But you do fit in at the London Victoria. Everyone in the department likes you.' He paused. This was a risk. The biggest one he'd taken yet with her. 'And I love you, Abby.'

She gave a mirthless laugh. 'If you love me, Lewis, why did you hurt me like that? Why did you dump me?'

'Because I'm an idiot. Because I was scared. And it was the worst decision I've ever made. I'm miserable without you. The world feels as if nothing's in the right place and nothing fits. I've never had that feeling before. When it ended with Jenna—yes, I was miserable, but I was sure I was doing the right thing. Since the day I broke up with you, I've been trying to convince myself that I made the right decision, and I know full well I didn't. I want you back, Abby.'

'If I say yes—' and she was giving him absolutely no clue about whether she was going to say yes or no '—how do I know you're not going to get cold feet and break up with me again?'

'I guess,' he said, 'I'm asking you to trust that I won't. I love you, and if you'll give me another chance then I'll learn to get over this ridiculous fear. With you by my side, I know I can do that.' He blew out a breath. 'I'll be honest, Abby. This scares me stupid. I want to do anything but sit here spilling my guts to you. I'd be happy to climb a mountain, walk over hot coals, swim through shark-infested waters. For me, talking about how I feel is harder and scarier than all of that put together.' He lifted his chin. 'So that's me done. What about you?'

'Me?' Abigail stared at him, not comprehending.

'How do you feel about me?' he asked. 'Because I really don't have a clue.'

Now he was challenging her to meet him halfway. To tell him how she felt.

To risk being rejected again.

'I thought,' she said carefully, 'that things were working out between us. I know I'm not particularly brave. I'm dull and quiet and the only interesting thing about me is that I'm Keith Brydon's daughter. But I thought you liked me for who I was.'

'I do,' he said softly.

'And I thought…with you, I could be brave. I thought I could risk telling you who I was. That it wouldn't matter and you'd still see me for who I am.'

He reached out and took her hand. 'I do see you, Abby. I see the woman who's quiet and serious and shy, but who's brave enough to go way out of her comfort zone whenever I've asked her to. I see the woman whose eyes have stormy circles round them when she's angry and whose cheeks have dimples when she's happy. I see,' he said, 'the woman who makes me see things in a different way. With you, I don't need the adrenalin stuff. You make my world feel complete. I love you, Abby.'

Abigail swallowed hard. 'Saying this isn't easy.'

He waited. And the hope in his eyes was enough to give her the courage she needed.

'I love you, Lewis,' she said.

'Even though I sometimes make stupid decisions?'

'Even though you sometimes make *very* stupid decisions,' she agreed. 'I see a man,' she said softly, 'who's more committed than anyone I've ever met. Who put his life on hold to keep his family together, and who even now tries to build bridges. I see a man who makes out that he's as shallow as a puddle and doesn't care, but he spends time with patients who've got nobody and he looks out for the vulnerable ones, having a quiet word with the right people to make sure they get the help and support they need. I see,' she said, 'the man I want to take a risk with.'

'I want to take a risk with you, too,' he said. 'I want commitment. I want you back, Abby. For now and for always. And I want the world to know that you're mine.'

'So you're suggesting we go public about the fact we're seeing each other?'

He shook his head. 'More than that. I want the whole deal. Marriage. A family.'

Everything she wanted.

Everything he'd said he didn't.

'But—I thought you didn't want marriage and a family? You said you felt trapped when you thought Jenna was pregnant.'

'Because I was twenty-three and ready to start my

life. I'm older now. Settled in my career. And,' he pointed out, 'you're not Jenna.'

'And you've already sort of done it, bringing your sisters up.'

'That was different, and I don't regret what I did—if I could rewind time and do it all over again, I'd still take those gap years and stick by my family. I wouldn't change that.' He wrinkled his nose. 'Except I'd do it with the benefit of hindsight and get my mum some proper help a lot earlier than she got it.'

He was really close to his sisters. And Abigail's old fears of not fitting in rose up to choke her. 'What if your family doesn't like me?'

'They will. You're nerdy enough for Dani and Ronnie to adore you, and Manda will love the fact that you take me to art galleries and Shakespeare. They'll love you,' he said simply. 'I can't make any guarantees about my mum. She might give you the cold shoulder. But don't take it personally—she's like that with everyone.' He looked thoughtfully at her. 'But I've seen you get through to the most uncommunicative patient at work. I have a feeling you might just be able to get through to her.'

'I can try,' Abigail said.

'What if your dad doesn't like me?' he asked.

She coughed. 'I've already talked to him about you.'

Lewis blew out a breath. 'If he knows how much I've hurt you, he'll want to take me apart. Which is pretty much how I feel about anyone who ever hurts you. Or our children.'

'He doesn't know that. And he doesn't need to know. He'll take you for who you are. If anything, I think you'll be horribly bad influences on each other and egg each other on to do mad things.' She stroked his face. 'You say you want children. What if we can't have them?'

'Then we can adopt. Or foster.' His eyes glittered. 'Actually, I know that foster-care is a lot better now than it was when I was a kid. And I'd quite like to be part of that.'

'Taking risks?'

He nodded. 'Teaching kids who've had a rough deal that life doesn't have to be that way. That everyone deserves a second chance.'

She could understand that. 'That works for me. I'll go with you on that.'

He smiled. 'Part of me wants to do this in a much more spectacular place, but you've taught me that I don't need all the trappings.' He dropped to one knee. 'Cinnamon Abigail Brydon Smith, I love you and I want to spend the rest of my life with you. Will you marry me?'

She could see in his eyes that he meant it. He really did want the whole thing with her. Marriage, a family, forever.

'Yes.'

He whooped, then in one single move stood up and scooped her up, whirling her round in the middle of her living room. And then he let her slide down his body until her feet touched the floor; he held her close, lowered his face to hers and kissed her. What started out slow and sweet and soft quickly turned heated; he kissed her as if he were starved for her.

When he broke the kiss, he was shaking. 'I love you, Abby.'

'I love you, too.'

'And I can't wait to get married to you.'

There was a suspicious gleam in his eyes, which made her back away. 'Lewis, don't get any bright ideas about skydiving with me to the wedding reception.'

He laughed. 'You wouldn't be allowed to jump out of a plane in your wedding dress. Unless, of course,' he said thoughtfully, 'you wear an orange jumpsuit as your wedding outfit. That would work.'

'No.' She laughed. 'I think I'd rather wear something that doesn't clash with my hair.'

'You looked cute. But I guess on our wedding day you'd rather have a tiara than a safety helmet.' He kissed her lingeringly. 'Besides, I don't need the adrenalin stuff with you.'

'I'm not going to stop you doing it,' she said. 'I might choose to watch you from the ground rather than join in with you every time, but I won't stop you doing something that makes you happy.'

'You make me happy,' he said softly. 'And I intend to do the same for you. For the rest of our days.'

* * * * *

Special Offers

Every month we put together collections and longer reads written by your favourite authors.

Here are some of next month's highlights— and don't miss our fabulous discount online!

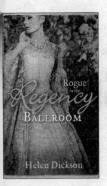

On sale 2nd August

On sale 2nd August

On sale 19th July

Save 20%
on all Special Releases

Join the Mills & Boon Book Club

Subscribe to **Medical** today for
3, 6 or 12 months and you could
save over £40!

We'll also treat you to these fabulous extras:

- FREE L'Occitane gift set worth £10

- FREE home delivery

- Rewards scheme, exclusive offers...and much more!

Subscribe now and save over £40
www.millsandboon.co.uk/subscribeme